RAINA

RAINA

A PREQUEL TO JACQUELINE WILLOUGHBY

Schuyler Randall

indiepen

IndiePen, A Vedere Press Company

ISBN-13: 978-1-7329886-0-6
ISBN-10: 1-7329886-0-9

TABLE OF CONTENTS

ACKNOWLEDGEMENTS

FIRST AND FOREMOST, I would like to thank God. He has given me the power to believe in my passion and pursue my dreams. I could never have done this without the faith I have in Him, the Almighty.

A very special thank you to my wife, Yvette, for her continued encouragement and understanding, and to my children and grandchildren.

Thank you to Gwen Marshall and Dr. Juanita Ayers, for taking time out of their busy lives to read a fledgling manuscript and offer invaluable advice.

Thank you to Anthony Vacca who gave me invaluable advice, encouragement, and positivity while working on this project.

Thank you to Shawn Crawford, Andrew and Dana Hill, Rod and Stephanie Gilcrest, and Mark Holley.

Thank you to my cousin Jacoby who reminds me of my childhood years.

A special thanks to my aunts Gwen, Nelta, Valerie, Vera, and Terry, and my uncle Jake.

Thank you to Write My Wrongs Editing and Vedere Press.

PROLOGUE

"What a pretty little girl, Frank," Jacqueline says to her husband.

"Yes, I agree, honey. God has blessed us," says Frank with a big grin on his face.

"Did you know," she starts, catching the midwife's attention, "that her name means queen?"

The midwife smiles and says, "No, I didn't know that. Her name is lovely."

Jacqueline gently lifts the newborn from the arms of the sleeping mother and holds the tiny bundle close to her with so much love.

Frank says, "Raina is our little queen."

Jacqueline stands up from the rocking chair in the baby's room and hands her to Frank to hold. Frank takes the baby in his arms and stands there like a statue.

"Relax, Frank, she won't break," says Jacqueline. "Sit down in the rocking chair. Just turn around and sit down." She laughs.

Frank slowly turns and sits down in the rocking chair. "She is so precious, so pretty," Frank says.

Jacqueline bends down and kisses Frank on the cheek; her long black hair, pinned up and away from her high cheekbones,

tickles his nose. She straightens up her slim body as she continues to gaze down on her child with bright, warm eyes and a
radiant, beautiful smile on her face. She is an educated, kind,
helpful, God-fearing woman who is loved by everyone.

The Willoughbys hire a nanny named Dora for Raina because they had just moved to Birmingham. Due to an increas-
ingly booming city, demand for lawyers in Birmingham brought
Frank and his family to a new home.

Jacqueline is busy returning to her work as a librarian and
contributing articles for the local newspaper, *The Birmingham
Post-Herald.*

Frank's sister Nancy had previously moved to Graysville,
Alabama from Pawley's Island, South Carolina. After graduating from nursing school, Nancy immediately began working at
Hillman Hospital as a nurse. Two years later, Nancy bought
herself a beautiful house a couple of miles from Frank and Jacqueline's home in Green Valley.

Raina starts school and enjoys it. She is always interacting
with the other kids, and she is full of delight. The teachers really
enjoy her outgoing personality and warm, loving spirit.

Once Raina starts the ninth grade in high school, with her
soothing and intelligent nature, Raina has a maturity that belies
her young age. She is athletic and very attractive with red hair
down to her shoulders, slim yet shapely figure, soft blue eyes, full
lips, shiny halo of white teeth, and height a little taller than the
average girl. During the first two years of high school, Raina
becomes very popular for her approachable personality, good
grades, social club involvements, athleticism, and her looks.

When not in school, she spends lots of time with her Aunt
Nancy sewing clothes, hand-painting all types of scenes, and
doing picture puzzles and arts and crafts for the different holidays to display in and outside of her house. Since she was a girl,

Nancy would play the piano and sing, and she soon discovers that Raina is a very talented singer. Nancy always dresses nicely, and with her beautiful black hair just past her shoulders, she's always complimented on her attractive appearance.

Nancy's love for hats and perfume rubbed off on Raina. They would spend time downtown, walking around and going to the different department stores like Pizitz's, Blach's, and—her favorite—Loveman's for its wondrous holiday décor. She basks in the intoxicating aromas of the high-end perfumes which she purchased only at those stores. Nancy is an avid reader of history and arts. Nancy and Raina read to each other and talk about past and present history, local government affairs, arts, and specific artists of the seventeenth century, which Nancy loves.

Chapter I

I SMILE

IT IS THE LAST WEEKEND IN MAY, right after Raina's sixteenth birthday, and she is spending the weekend with her Aunt Nancy. The two are putting together a picture puzzle at the kitchen table.

"Raina, I have a friend of mine coming over to take us to the movies this afternoon," says Nancy.

"Who is the friend?" asks Raina.

"He's one of the doctors doing his residency. We have become good friends, and he asked if I would go out with him. I said only if my niece can come along with us, and he gladly agreed," Nancy laughs.

Dr. James Posey, a young doctor from Boston, Massachusetts, arrives and walks up to Nancy and Raina sitting on the porch swing.

"Hello, ladies," Dr. Posey says. He has blonde hair, a slender body, wearing a pair of dress trousers with a short-sleeved two-pocket shirt, matching hat, and black leather shoes.

"Miss Nancy, this must be your pretty niece, Raina."

"Dr. Posey, you are correct," says Nancy.

"Hello, Raina, your name is very nice," says the young doctor.

"Thank you, Dr. Posey," replies Raina, who has a bright smile that could light up the night.

"The two of you look so much alike!" he remarks, eyes lingering on both of their faces for a moment before sending a grin to Raina. She blushes and flicks her eyes to Nancy whose lips curl up in amusement. He winks at both of them then takes a step backwards, pointing a thumb over his shoulder to the car. "Ready to go to the movies?"

"Yes, Dr. Posey, we're ready," answers Nancy.

As Raina and her aunt walk down the porch stairs to the doctor's car, she admires its maroon body and the tan convertible top, white wall tires, and shining chrome hubcaps.

"Nice ride," Nancy comments.

Dr. Posey grins. "Thanks. My father had a dickens of a time buying it for me, but the money was definitely worth it, wouldn't you say?"

Nancy agrees, and the doctor turns to the high schooler. "Miss Raina, you may get in," says the doctor.

"Thank you, Dr. Posey." She sits down, grinning the whole time and enjoying the politeness of the doctor. He then walks over to the passenger-side front door and opens it for Nancy who gets in and sits down with the look of a princess and the style of a perfect lady.

As they are on their way to the Five Points Theater, Dr. Posey and Nancy have a conversation about work. "Miss Nancy, how's everything going with the nurses on your floor?" he asks.

"All is good. All my nurses are busy taking care of our patients, and I feel we finally have the doctors convinced we can handle the workload. Dr. Davis is so nice to the staff and has the best bedside manner of any of the other doctors there. I enjoy working with him. His peers have the utmost respect for him, and the nurses enjoy working for him because of his excellent people skills," says Nancy.

"You're right. Dr. Davis is a wonderful man to work with. I'm very fortunate to have him as my supervisor. He teaches me something new every day," says James. "I'm glad that I'm not doing my residency under Dr. Christopher; he's such an arrogant old mule." They both laugh.

The three arrive at the Five Points Theater. Dr. Posey parks the car, gets out, and opens the door for both Nancy and Raina. The three stand in front of the movie theater with its green and white glass façade, a brightly lit marquee board outside, which reads, "Now Showing *The Wizard of Oz*, starring Judy Garland."

"I've been looking forward to seeing this," says Nancy.

"I think it should be a pretty good movie," says Raina.

"Well, let's gets some tickets and go into the theater," says Dr. Posey. The three walk up to the ticket box office, and Dr. Posey pays for three movie tickets. He steps over to the glass entrance doors to the theater's foyer and opens it.

"Ladies," he says as he extends his hand out, and the two walk into the foyer outside of the movie room.

As Nancy and James sit down in the foyer, Raina standing and looking at the posters of upcoming movies, someone comes up from behind and places their hands over her eyes.

"Guess who?" asks the excited voice of a young lady.

"Concepción!" answers Raina with her bright smile showing despite a hand over each eye.

Concepción steps around and says, "I saw you come in! Hi, Aunt Nancy, how are you doing?"

Concepción leans down and gives Nancy a hug. "I'm doing well, Concepción. I want to introduce you to Dr. Posey, a friend of mine from the hospital. Dr. Posey, this is Raina's best friend and a very close friend of the family, Concepción."

Dr. Posey stands and tips his hat and says, "Hello, Concepción. It's very nice to meet a pretty young lady with a unique name. What does it mean?"

Concepción replies, "It's nice to meet you, too, doctor, and thanks for the compliment. I'm named after a city southwest of Santiago in central Chile. My father visited when he was young and loved the name so much he said if he ever had a daughter, he would name her Concepción, so here I am."

Raina asks her, "Who's here at the movies with you?"

"I'm here with my parents who want to see *The Wizard of Oz*," said Concepción. "Raina, come sit in the movie with me."

Raina looks at her Aunt Nancy. "Would it be okay if I sit with Concepción in the movie? That would give you and Dr. Posey time without the third wheel."

Nancy smiles and looks at Dr. Posey then back at Raina and replies, "Yes, and we will meet you back out here when it's over. Third wheel, too funny!" Nancy laughs.

"Okay, Aunt Nancy," replies Raina.

"Nice meeting you, Dr. Posey, and see you later, Aunt Nancy," says Concepción as she grabs Raina's hand to get in line for popcorn and soda before the movie starts.

"We have a little time to talk before the movie starts," says Nancy, smiling at Dr. Posey on the bench in the lounging area of the theater.

"Miss Nancy, tell me more about yourself," says Dr. Posey.

"Okay, first, you can call me Nancy. We're not at work, and I'm not wearing all white," she grins. "I lived with my Aunt Louise for a few months, who was a wonderful God-fearing woman. She loved to dress and wear her lovely hats to church. She had a warm smile and a big heart; I miss her so much. Then later, I moved in with my brother Frank and his wife Jacqueline where I attended and finished high school. I got my nursing degree from the Hillman Hospital training school for nurses and stayed working at the hospital right after graduation. My mother was first a nurse before becoming a stay-at-home mother, and my father worked as an engineer for the railroad. But enough about me, Dr. Posey. Tell me about you," she offers with those beautiful blue eyes looking directly into James's.

"First, please call me James. Second, my father is a history professor at Holy Cross University and serves on the school board of directors and on the Boston city council," says James. "I always wanted to be a doctor, even as a kid. I was the one always administering the first aid to the kids in the community. I attended Harvard University, and now I'm here doing my residency."

"What made you move from Massachusetts to Alabama? Do you have any relatives here?"

"I heard Birmingham was growing and thought that this would be a great place to build my career. Unfortunately, I don't have any relatives here, but my father has a good childhood friend that moved here many years ago. He and his wife keep an eye on me," says James as he laughs. "But hopefully, I have a new close friend." James winks.

He notices a few patrons heading into the theater. "I see it's time to go, Nancy." He stands up and reaches his hand out for her. She takes it, and the two walk over to give their tickets to the attendant.

After two hours, Dr. Posey and Nancy come out of the movie.

"That was a very good movie. Would it be too soon to say that I'd want to see that again?" Nancy asks.

"I agree," replies James.

As the two enter back into the theater foyer, a voice comes out of the crowd, calling the doctor's name. The young doctor turns to his left, and a young gentleman steps up, reaching out and shaking James's hand.

"Nancy," James says excitedly. "I want you to meet a couple of friends of mine: Dale and Clarence." Both gentlemen say hello as they tilt their hats.

Nancy smiles, nods her head, and says, "Good evening, gentlemen."

"I haven't seen you guys since you both left the hospital," says James, excited to see his old friends. "What are you two doing these days?"

Dale replies, "We're at McWane Steel. We got jobs there right after leaving St. Vincent's. It's not what we went to school for, but it pays the bills."

James says, "Guys, it's so good to see the both of you."

James looks at Nancy, but she replies, "Go talk with your old friends. I'll sit here in the foyer until Raina and Concepción get out of the movie."

James smiles. "I will be right out front. Back in a couple of minutes." The three guys turn and head out the glass doors in front of the theater.

The three young men each light up a cigarette and begin talking.

Dale asks, "How's the residency at Hillman Hospital going, my friend?"

"It's going pretty well," says James. "I really miss you guys. It was so much fun when the three of us were starting our residency at St. Vincent's."

"Yes, old friend, those were good times back then," says Clarence.

"You make it seem so long ago, Clarence. What was it, about two years ago?" asks James.

"Yes, about two years ago. It was two years ago that our lives were changed."

James drops his head down and says, "You guys made a mistake; so what? I just don't understand why those old goats on the medical board won't let you guys practice medicine."

"Clarence and I wanted to save that sick boy's life, but we should have never given him that experimental medicine. It was hard to see him suffer. It was an unknown disease, but we had to do something. By administering the medicine to him, we broke the law, but thanks to your father, we didn't go to jail. He got us out of that mess to give us a fresh start, but we will never get the opportunity to practice medicine again," Dale finishes solemnly.

Noticing the frown on his friend's face, Dale clears his throat and plasters a grin on. "Enough about us," he says then lightly bumps a fist on James's arm. "Who's the pretty little lady you're with?"

"That's Nancy Willoughby, a nurse at the hospital. We are on a date, along with her niece Raina. Nancy is a wonderful lady. We talk at the hospital, so I asked her out, and here we are on our first date."

Clarence looks at James and asks, "Does she know why you are in Birmingham and not Boston?"

He grips both of their shoulders and flicks his dark gaze between them. "Do not," he growls, "*do not*—tell anyone." His hands tighten. "Understand?"

James takes in a deep breath and slowly releases them. Clarence says, "I will never tell a soul, but we know what you've done in Boston, and we don't want it to happen again, good friend." He is looking directly into James's eyes, and he places his hand on James's shoulder.

"It won't happen again, Clarence. I have it under control," James says. His fingers drum a chaotic beat on his crossed arms. "I have it under control."

Clarence continues to hold his gaze, and James shifts his

weight between his feet until he finally breaks the stare and chuckles nervously.

"Hey, guys, it was good to see the both of you. I'm glad you both are doing okay, but I've got to head back in, alright?"

Dale replies, proud of his friend, "Good to see you, too, Dr. James Posey."

"Good to have run into you and had the chance to talk," says Clarence, scrutinizing James.

Dale steps over and gives James a handshake and a hug. He then says, "Take care, buddy. Here is our house address and phone number. Don't be a stranger, doctor."

Clarence steps up and gives James a handshake and a hug. "Proud of you, man. Keep moving forward and become the best doctor in Alabama," he says. The two friends hold each other's gaze before, finally, Clarence closes his eyes and sighs, his entire body deflating with that exhale. A moment later, he straightens up and his tired yet stern eyes lock with James. "James, you're not well." He stares imploringly at him. "Get some help."

James looks at Clarence as if he's a kid being counseled by a teacher. Clarence then changes his facial expression to a friendly smile and says, "It was good seeing you today, James. You have our address, so don't be a stranger. Please let Nancy know it was a pleasure meeting her."

"Will do." James stands, watching them walk away, then he turns and goes back into the theater's foyer to Nancy.

As James approaches, he sees that Raina and Concepción are standing with her.

"I'm back, Nancy. Thank you for being understanding and patient while I spoke with my old friends."

Nancy beams at James. "No problem. This gave us girls a chance to talk." Both Raina and Concepción laugh.

"Would you ladies have been talking about me by chance?"

James asks, chuckling. He then looks down at his watch and says, "Looks like the evening is still young. Would you care to have dinner?"

"That would be very nice of you, James," says Nancy.

"I would love to go get something to eat," says Raina.

"Raina, will your friend be joining us?" asks James.

Concepción looks at Raina and replies, "Thank you for the invite, but my parents and I are going to the Irondale Café."

"Okay, it was good seeing you, Concepción," says Nancy.

"You too." She gives Nancy a hug and reaches her hand to shake Dr. Posey's, saying, "It was very nice to meet you, Dr. Posey."

"It was good to meet you, too."

Concepción then gives Raina a hug and says, "I'll see you at church tomorrow." They wave to each other, and the remaining group heads to the car.

As the three are headed to the car, James says, "I know of a very good restaurant in Bessemer named The Bright Star. I heard it has some of the best food around. I've been trying to get down there and try the food, but I've never had anyone that wanted to go with me."

"Well, James, I have no problem going with you, and I think Raina has no problem going either," says Nancy as she looks at James with her glowing personality that can brighten the darkest day.

"Sounds good." James opens the car doors for each of the ladies before getting into the driver's side and heading toward Bessemer.

During dinner, the three have a wonderful time talking about the Willoughby family and James's family.

James asks Raina, "So, I hear you are entering your senior year in high school. What are your plans next?"

"I'm going to attend Hillman Nursing School and become a nurse like my aunt."

James replies, "Excellent idea! I heard the Hillman and Jefferson Hospitals are going to merge, which will make the need for more good nurses like your Aunt Nancy.

"What else can you tell me about yourself, Raina? Do you have a lot of friends? Do you have a boyfriend?" asks James.

With an instant blush, she looked over at her Aunt Nancy. "Yes, I have a lot of good friends, and yes, I have a boyfriend. His name is Alexander. He's a very nice and polite guy. He really likes me a lot."

Nancy smiles. "Raina, you never mentioned you had a boyfriend. How long have you been seeing Alexander?"

"About three months," Raina replies.

"Do your parents know about him?"

"My mother does, but I haven't mentioned him to Dad. I'm actually going to ask my parents if he can come over and meet them."

"Is he in school or does he work?"

"Both. He's a freshman at Birmingham Southern College, and he works at Loveman's department store," says Raina, showing her beautiful, bright smile. "He wants to get his degree in business because he wants to run a big company someday."

"He sounds like a good guy, Raina. I wish you two the best," says James.

After dessert, James pays the tab, leaves a nice tip, and they leave to go back to Nancy's house.

Chapter II

IF TROUBLE DON'T COME TODAY

THEY ARRIVE BACK TO NANCY'S HOUSE AROUND EIGHT. James opens the car doors for the girls and walks them to the front door.

"I really enjoyed our day together. I hope the two of you did," says James from his place on the steps. Raina takes her key out of her purse and opens the door.

"James, I hope you'll come in for a little while, unless you are tired and want to get home," Nancy says as she winks at James.

"Well, I guess I can stay just a little while," James says. Raina just smiles at both of them and goes into the house.

Nancy turns and walks in as James follows behind. As they walk into the living room, Nancy says, "James, please have a seat."

James thanks her and sits down on the couch. As James sits, looking around and admiring the nicely decorated living room, he says, "You have a very nice home, Nancy."

"Thank you," Nancy replies. "Let me put my purse and hat away, and I'll be back in a minute." She goes down the hall into her bedroom for a minute and returns back to the living room.

Raina comes back into the room and says, "Aunt Nancy, I'm going to give Alexander a quick call, take a bath, do some homework, and go to bed." She turns to their guest. "Dr. Posey, I had a wonderful time today! Thank you so much for taking us to the movies and to a very nice dinner." She walks over, leans down, and gives James a hug.

He replies, "You are welcome. I hope to see you next year in nursing school and working at the hospital." Raina smiles then goes over and gives her aunt a hug, wishes both a good night with a kiss on the cheek, and leaves the room.

Raina retreats to Nancy's bedroom and shuts the door. She sits down in the chair across the room where the telephone sits on a small table. She picks up the phone to call Alexander, and his mother answers.

"Mrs. Mitchell, may I speak to Alexander, please?"

"Hello, Raina, good to hear your voice. I will get him."

After a brief moment, Alexander answers. "Hello," he says. "How was your day?"

She tells him about the movie and dinner, then she asks about his work.

"It was good, busy, which made time go by. Raina, I thought about you all day. I look forward to seeing you at church tomorrow."

"I miss you, too," says Raina. She pauses and twirls the phone cord around her finger.

"Alexander," she starts hesitantly, voice soft. She bites her lip a moment and shifts in her seat. "Do you...do you like me?"

"Yes."

"Tell me you love me," Raina requests in a very sincere and sensual voice.

"I love you, Raina."

"I love you, too, Alexander. Good night."

"Good night and sweet dreams."

Raina hangs the phone up and sits there for a moment,

thinking about how nice of a guy Alexander is. She smiles, goes to the bathroom and runs her bath water. She takes a hot bath, gets herself dressed for bed, sits down at the vanity in the guest bedroom, and brushes her hair. Once done, she sits and reads for a little while, walks over to the bed, kneels down, and says her prayers. Once she finishes praying, she gets into bed. Raina falls asleep with a smile on her face, thinking about her wonderful day with Nancy and James and her boyfriend she loves.

———

Nancy returns to the living room to sit down on the couch next to James. She brings two glasses and a bottle of wine and places them on the coffee table. "Would you like to have a glass of wine with me, James?"

"I probably shouldn't," he replies reluctantly.

"Just one glass," she cajoles, clinking the empty glasses together. When he doesn't respond, she sighs and sets the glasses back down on the table. "Well, if you don't want any, that's fine. I'll put it away."

"No, Nancy, I will have one glass," he says before she can get up. Nancy hands James the bottle of wine and the cork screw. He opens it and pours a little in each glass and sets the bottle down on the coffee table. He then picks up both glasses, handing one to Nancy.

"Let's do a toast," he says. "Here's to all the staff at Hillman Hospital." The two touch glasses, and they take a sip.

As the night continues, the two talk about the hospital staff members, nurses on Nancy's floor, the different doctors' personalities, their experiences, and the patients. They laugh about each other's upbringing, Nancy growing up in the south and James being from up north. They discuss different dialects, food, cultures, and different religious faiths—southern Baptist and Catholic.

After taking another sip of wine, James asks, "Nancy, why is a very smart, independent, and beautiful woman like yourself single?"

Nancy pulls the wine glass from her lips and pauses, clearing her throat while expressing a blushing smile. "I guess I'm very particular with who I want to court me. I want to marry the man of my dreams. I want him to be smart, successful, very sociable, like art and music, enjoy being around family and friends, especially because I want kids. I also want him to be a Christian. My church is so important to me, so I want to be able to share that part of my life with him."

"I understand," he replies as he slowly nods his head, agreeing.

"Now, what are you looking for in a woman?"

"All the traits you just mentioned."

James puts his wine glass on the coffee table and slides over closer to Nancy who was sitting back comfortably on the couch. "You are the most beautiful woman I have ever seen," he says.

"Thank you." Nancy blushes, holding her wine glass with both hands. James reaches over and takes the wine glass from her hands, placing it on the coffee table. He then leans over and kisses Nancy on her lips. They look into each other's eyes and begin to slowly deepen the kiss. James puts his arms around her, and Nancy encircles her arms around his neck. The two passionately kiss, but James becomes a little aggressive while kissing and feeling on Nancy. Nancy lifts up from the couch, politely pushing James back. James then pushes her hand back, still kissing her.

Nancy turns her head away and says in a low voice, "Okay, James, that's enough."

James then starts back kissing her. Again, Nancy says,

"Enough, James!" as she tries to push him away with both hands. "James, stop it!" Nancy says in a stern voice. But James is now being more aggressive.

Nancy then slaps James across the face with a look of disgust. "Stop!"

The slap turns James's head away from her face, and he stops.

"Please leave now!" Nancy demands.

James whips his head back to Nancy, a menacing sneer distorting his features.

Nancy scrambles up, clutching her now wrinkled dress in a shaking hand. She backs away from his manic gaze and trains her wide eyes on him.

Then, out of nowhere, James rears back and punches Nancy on the chin, knocking her onto the couch before she rolls onto the floor. He slowly stalks toward her, disheveled hair casting an engulfing shadow over his eyes, and she can only see the manic tilt of his lips as he approaches her.

Raina, down the hall, startles awake when she hears a shattering crash.

She quickly gets out of bed and runs down the hall, screaming, "Aunt Nancy!"

As she enters into the living room, James is on top of Nancy, trying to hold her down as she fights and screams for help.

Raina shrieks, "Stop! Get off my aunt!"

Raina runs up and jumps on James's back, grabbing him around the neck and biting him on the side of the face. James yells, and he reaches up to grab a handful of hair. He pulls Raina off his back while she is swinging and hitting him in the chest and face. He drags her up by the hair and tightens his free hand around her throat, now releasing her hair to punch her in the face. Her head snaps back against the wall, and she slumps to the floor, unconscious.

James turns around to Nancy lying on the floor. She's scared, shaking, and her face is scratched and bruised, her eyes swollen.

"Please don't hurt me. Please don't hurt me." She sobs.

James walks toward her, unfazed by Nancy's plea. The sickness that Clarence mentioned hours earlier has surfaced. James can't control his temper, and he beats Nancy.

Over an hour later, Raina wakes up on the floor. She lifts her head up and looks over across the torn-up living room to see Aunt Nancy sitting in the corner of the room, beaten and bruised. She is in shock, just looking straight ahead, her lips moving but no words coming out.

Raina gets up, the right side of her cheek bruised with a little blood on the corner of her mouth. She walks over, crying, and gets down on the floor next to Nancy. She puts her arm around her and says, "It's going to be alright, auntie. I'm going to go get help." Raina runs to the telephone and calls her father.

Frank arrives at Nancy's house. He runs in through the front door, yelling, "Raina, Nancy, where are you?"

He looks over in the corner of the living room and says, "Oh my God."

He kneels down in front of Nancy who is still on the floor, with Raina holding her dear aunt.

"What happened, Raina?" asks Frank.

"Dr. Posey assaulted her, Dad! That man beat her!" Raina cries.

"Nancy, are you okay?" asks Frank as he pushes Nancy's hair back, looking at the bruises on her face and her black, swollen eyes.

"Raina, are *you* okay?" Frank asks once he notices the side of Raina's face is red and swollen.

"Yes, Dad, I'm alright."

Frank turns to Nancy. "Come on and stand up, sister." He then slowly stands with his arm under Nancy's arm, and she slowly follows. Raina is on the other side, helping her aunt to her feet.

The two on each side of her walk over toward the couch, but Nancy screams, "No!" Instead, Raina gets a chair out of the kitchen and sits her down.

"Raina, did you call the police?" he asks.

"Yes, Dad, I called the police."

"Raina," says Frank, "make sure you tell the police everything that happened. I know of James Posey's father, and he is a powerful man. I want to make sure we get his son locked up for good for putting his hands on my sister and my daughter."

"Yes, sir," Raina agrees, still crying. Frank walks back over and puts his arms around his sister. Raina follows and puts her arms around Nancy as well. More tears stream down her face, and she continues to silently mumble to herself.

They can hear the sirens of the police cars and the fire brigade as they arrive at the house. They place Nancy on the stretcher and put her in the ambulance to take her to the hospital. Raina walks away from the officers and Frank to get into the ambulance with Nancy.

Frank calls Jacqueline and says, "Get to the hospital. Nancy is being admitted, and I will explain everything once you get there."

Once Frank arrives at the hospital, he speaks with the police and explains what happened. He let Raina speak with the policeman taking the report, and she tells him that Dr. James Posey had assaulted Aunt Nancy.

Officer Baker tries to get a statement from Nancy, but she is deeply in shock.

———

James flees the house after the terrible crime he committed.

"What the hell did I just do!? I can't believe this has happened again," he shrieks as he frantically drives. He drives about ten miles down the road and sees a phone booth, so he stops. He makes a collect long-distance call to Boston. The operator connects, and James's father answers the phone.

"Hello, James. Why are you calling so late? Are you doing okay?" his dad asks.

"Dad, it happened again! It happened again! I don't know what came over me! Please help me, Dad!" James cries, slowly sliding down to squat in the phone booth.

"James, pull yourself together. Pull yourself together, son. Go to a friend's house for now and stay there. I will catch the first flight to Birmingham in the morning. You got that, James?"

"Yes, Dad." He sobs.

"I'm going to call my friend, Judge Roberts. Find a friend's house to stay at until I get there. Call your mother and let her know where you are in the morning, and I will call her to find out where you are as soon as I get there."

"Okay, Dad, please get here as fast as you can."

"I will, son."

James stays squatting for about two minutes, then he stands up and hangs up the phone. He reaches into his pants pocket and pulls out the address Dale gave him earlier. He gets back into the car and drives to his old friend's rented house in Norwood.

James arrives in front of the house that Dale and Clarence rent. He runs up the stairs and knocks on the door.

James runs a shaking hand through his hair as he waits. He can hear muffled shuffling and voices. They become louder, until he hears, "Who is it?"

"It's me, Clarence," says James urgently and nervously.

Clarence opens the door, and James enters right in. "What happened, James? You look terrible."

James's hair is disheveled, the front of his shirt is torn and buttons are gone, scratches blemish his face and neck, and a bite mark covers his left cheek. James quickly collapses into the nearest chair in the living room.

James has his face in his hands. "It happened again, Clarence. I couldn't control myself," he cries and looks up at Clarence. "I'm going to prison this time. I don't know what came over me. I'm so sorry." He puts his face back in his hands and starts heavily crying.

Clarence sits down in front of James. "Was it that Nancy woman?"

"Yes! We were kissing, and she told me to stop, and I got angry; I lost my mind, Clarence! She slapped me, and I started hitting her again and again. I was so angry, but I couldn't stop, Clarence. I couldn't stop!" James breaks down crying even more.

Clarence wishes he would've warned that woman, Nancy, at the theater, but he stupidly hoped James wouldn't do anything, that his friend actually wasn't responsible for what happened in Boston. How wrong he was.

"Did you call your father?" asks Clarence.

"Yes, he said to get to a friend's house and stay put until he gets in town."

"Okay, Dale is at work right now," says Clarence. "Where is your car?"

"It's outside."

"I'm going to take it a couple of blocks over and park it."

"Okay, thanks," says James.

"I'm sure the police are looking for you, so let me get the car out of here," says Clarence. He knows covering for the doctor is wrong, but he feels obligated to James. When he and Dale were in trouble, James helped. He wants to return the favor.

He grabs the car keys from James's jacket and his hat off the coat rack before urgently walking out the door. James sits forward in the living room chair with his face in his hands and says, "God, help me."

The next day, James's father arrives in Birmingham at Clarence and Dale's place with the big-time attorney Jed Murphy. The three sit down and review the details of what happened the previous night at Nancy's house. After about four hours of talking and counseling, they finally decide on a plan.

"Mr. Posey," Murphy says, "we are going down to the police station to let James turn himself in then immediately get bail set. Then, we will go from there."

As the three men are leaving to go to the police station, James says, "Thank you so much, Clarence and Dale, for letting me stay here. You both put yourselves in danger for me."

"Good friend, you were there when we needed you, so we could only repay you," says Clarence.

The two shake hands, and Mr. Posey says, "Thank you, gentlemen, for looking out for my boy. I will repay you once we get all this cleared up."

"You're welcome," says Clarence and Dale as they shake Mr. Posey's hand.

The three gentlemen arrive at the police station and go to the front desk after a quick drive in Murphy's car. Attorney Murphy starts explaining that they were there for Dr. James Posey to turn himself in. The police officers take James to the back and start the booking process. He is charged with the assault of a minor and felonious assault of Nancy Willoughby. He is taken into the interrogation room and questioned. Once the officers finish interrogating him, James is arrested and taken to a holding cell.

A couple of hours later at the arraignment hearing, Dr. James Posey is charged with the crimes and pleads not guilty. The judge sets the bail amount, which Mr. Posey pays, and his son is released. The preliminary hearing is scheduled in two weeks.

Chapter III

I DON'T KNOW WHY

AFTER THREE DAYS IN THE HOSPITAL, Nancy is released to go home. She is physically well, but mentally scarred.

Frank, Jacqueline, and Raina are at the hospital to take Nancy home, but she tells Jacqueline she doesn't want to go back to her house. Jacqueline tells Nancy she is welcome to stay at their house as long as she wants.

Most of the nurses that work with Nancy come by the room and hug her and say they are looking forward to her coming back when she is fully well. Her favorite, Doctor Davis, comes by the room and tells her how much of a wonderful and strong nurse she is and to take all the time she needs off. He tells her, "You are the best nurse, by far, that I have ever worked with."

After about three weeks, Nancy seems headed in the right direction for mental recovery. She is socializing with family and friends that come over to the house to see her. She helps Dora cook and clean around the house and work in the flower garden, and she's back doing arts and crafts. There are no issues until Raina asks her Aunt Nancy to go for a ride with her to go shopping. Nancy agrees, but when she walks out to the car, she freezes. Her face is stuck in a terrified stare, and she shakes nervously.

"What's wrong, Aunt Nancy?" Raina asks.

She stands there for a moment, never saying a word, then she turns and walks back into the house. Raina gets out of the car and follows her aunt inside.

"Aunt Nancy, what's wrong?" Raina asks again.

Aunt Nancy sits down in the living room, holding herself, just looking into space. Raina goes into the kitchen where Jacqueline and Dora are baking cakes.

"Mother, can you go speak with Aunt Nancy? Something is wrong," says Raina.

"Of course," Jacqueline replies, putting down the cake icing spatula and taking off her apron. "Stay here, Raina, and help Dora finish icing the cakes. I'll be back in a minute."

As she enters the room, Nancy is sitting in the chair, straight as a board and in a daze.

"How are you feeling, Nancy?" Jacqueline asks. Nancy doesn't say a word, so she walks over to sit in the wingback chair next to her and asks again, "Are you feeling alright, Nancy?"

About twenty seconds later, Nancy replies, "I don't want to go anywhere. I'm scared. I don't want to leave the house. I don't want to ever go back to my house. I don't want to go to work. I don't want to see anyone, and I don't want anything anymore, Jacqueline. I hate him for what he did to me!" Nancy starts crying. "I don't want anyone to look at me. That bastard took my life."

Jacqueline stands up and wraps her arms around Nancy, telling her, "Everything will be alright. You can't let what happened ruin your life. You have to fight back and refuse to let someone have power over you. You have to fight! Nancy, you have to hold your head up, pull your shoulders back, and move forward with life. You have your family, friends, and patients who are depending on you to come back stronger than ever.

Raina needs you, Nancy."

Nancy looks up at Jacqueline with tears running down her face and says, "I messed up once, and my parents sent me off because they didn't want their image tarnished and for me to look like a whore. Once I had the baby..." Raina gasps, hands still sticky from the icing she planned to sneak by and wash off, now eavesdropping. "I didn't want to give her away, but I was able to finish high school and college and, most importantly, be around my child. Now, again, I have messed up, and you two are there for me again."

Nancy stands up, reaches outs, and the two ladies hug. Then Nancy stands back and says, "I don't know about this, Jacqueline. I don't know if I can get past this one."

Nancy turns and walks out the front door and sits on the front porch, deep in thought. Jacqueline walks over to the couch, sits down, and says to herself, "The day has come. I think it's time that Frank, Nancy, and I have a talk about telling Raina the truth."

———

Two weeks later at the preliminary hearing, Judge Roberts is presiding to listen to evidence and testimony from the defendant's attorney and the prosecuting attorney. Frank has a good friend and attorney named George Proctor. Attorney Proctor is well respected in the south, as well as one of the top lawyers. Attorney Proctor has prosecuted and won many cases over his fifteen year career as an attorney. Raina is at the preliminary hearing, but Nancy is not mentally able to attend.

After all the evidence and testimonies are heard, Judge Roberts determines that there is enough evidence to believe the defendant committed the crimes.

Attorney Murphy stands before the judge and enters a plea of no contest for his client. Judge Roberts sets a date for one week to sentence the defendant for the crime.

A week later in Judge Roberts' courtroom, Dr. James Posey stands in front of the judge with Attorney Murphy next to him to receive his sentencing.

"Dr. Posey, you are hereby sentenced two years' probation, and you have an order to be admitted to a mental facility in Boston, Massachusetts. Your medical license will be suspended until further notice. This court is adjourned."

Dr. Posey shakes Attorney Murphy's hand and says, "Thank you!"

"Great job, Murphy," Mr. Posey says while shaking his hand next. He turns to James. "Son, let's get you packed and back to Boston."

The three head out of the courtroom. As they are walking down the aisle, Dr. Posey looks over at a disappointed Raina and takes his eyes off her quickly, turning his head away in shame. Raina, watching him, cries not tears of hurt but tears of hatred.

She silently mouths to him, "You will pay."

Raina keeps looking at Dr. Posey even after he had turned away, and is now shaking hands on his way out of the courtroom.

Attorney Proctor and Frank are outraged over the verdict.

"What the hell just happened, George?" Frank asks.

"I don't believe what I just heard, either. I will file a motion for an appeal, as soon as possible," Attorney Proctor says, displeased over the sentencing.

After leaving the court house, the ride home is very quiet. Raina just looks out the passenger side window in deep thought, a frown marring her face and her interlocked hands clenched.

Once the two arrive at the house, Raina retreats to her room. Frank finds Jacqueline writing a letter at the desk in the study.

"Frank, I didn't want to hear the news at work, so I came home. What was the outcome? How many years did Dr. Posey get?" asks Jacqueline.

"He got two-year's probation and an order back to Boston to be admitted into a mental hospital."

"What!? Are you serious?" She removes her reading glasses and looks at Frank in disbelief.

"I'm just as shocked as you are, Jacqueline. The judge agreed that Dr. Posey, being diagnosed with an aggressive personality type, needed to go back to Boston to receive psychiatric treatment. Being a doctor with a good reputation stopped him from going to prison, even though we found out this is not his first assault victim. The victims would not testify against him, though. His father persuaded them to change their minds."

"If this was presented to Judge Roberts, why isn't he locked up?" asks Jacqueline.

Frank stares above Jacqueline's head for a moment with a very serious look, then looks back down at her and says, "Jacqueline, Mr. Posey knows the judge personally."

———

Raina goes up to her room and closes her bedroom door. She walks over and sits at the window seat, looking into the backyard that has a view of the forest.

A couple of hours later, there is a knock at Raina's bedroom door. The door opens and Concepción enters.

"Raina, my mother got a call. I heard the news and came right over," says Concepción. Raina stands up, and her best friend gives her a hug. "I'm so sorry. He doesn't deserve to be free."

"Concepción, he has to pay for this," says Raina as she turns and sits back down on the window seat.

Concepción then grabs Raina's hand and says, "Come on, let's go over to my house." Raina is pulled up, and she follows her friend out of the bedroom to go to her house.

As they are leaving, Raina calls to Dora, who is watering plants in the living room. "Dora, I'm going over to Concepción's house for a little while. I'll be back later this evening."

As the two girls walk out through the front screen door, Aunt Nancy is sitting on the front porch in the swing, staring into space.

"Hello, Miss Nancy," greets Concepción. Nancy does not respond. She just keeps looking at nothing.

"Aunt Nancy, Concepción just said hello," Raina says as she walks over to Nancy to put her hand on Nancy's shoulder, kneeling down.

Nancy looks at Raina with a smile and says, "Hi."

Raina kisses her aunt and says, "I'm going with Concepción to her house for a little while. I'll be back soon." She stands up and walks down the porch steps, looking back at her aunt, who is slowly drifting into depression. The two girls get into Concepción's car and drive off, but Raina still watches her aunt as she fades in the distance and wonders when she will mentally recover from the tragic event.

Chapter IV

IT'S TIME

RAINA STARTS HER SENIOR YEAR OF HIGH SCHOOL. She is very excited and, of course, a very popular girl. She averages an A in her academics, she is captain of the girls' tennis team, and co-captain of the chess team. She is also the most beautiful girl in the high school.

On a Monday evening in February, Raina returns home from school. In the car that Frank bought her at the beginning of the school year, she pulls up in the driveway. She gets her books off the front seat, gets out of the car, and goes into the house. "Good evening, everyone," she greets as she walks through the door. She's unclasping her shoes when she notices her father, and she startles. "Dad, what are you doing home so early?" Raina asks with curiosity.

Frank replies, "We need to talk. We have something we need to tell you. Please have a seat next to Nancy."

Raina places her books on the coffee table and sits down next to her Aunt Nancy on the couch. Frank is sitting in one chair that's across from Nancy, and Jacqueline is sitting in the other chair next to Frank.

Nancy turns to face Raina. "Please give me your hands."

Raina gives Nancy her hands, and she holds them, looking

right into Raina's eyes. "Raina, sweetie," Nancy starts, "this may be difficult or strange for you to hear, but...when I was a teen, I was pregnant." Nancy pauses a moment to gauge Raina's reaction, but she merely looks expectant, waiting for the rest, so she continues. "I was pregnant, and I ended up having a child, but I gave that child to my brother to raise." She swipes a lock of Raina's red hair behind her ears. "Raina, I'm your mother."

Raina catches Nancy's hand on the way down and grips it tightly in her own. Raina's eyes are filled with tears, but they don't fall down her face.

Raina sits there for a few seconds in silence, then she says, "I know. A few months ago, when you were afraid to get in the car to go shopping, I was eavesdropping. I overhead you and mother talking, and you mentioned having a baby. I wondered why we looked so much alike, and after hearing that conversation, I knew it was me."

Jacqueline asks, "Why haven't you said anything about it to us?"

"I had to think about it. I realized I'm very happy to have been raised by all three of you. I didn't care because inside my heart, Aunt Nancy is my mother, too."

Nancy's heart fills with joy as she says, "Yes, my lovely daughter, I'm your mother." The two hug, and tears of joy run down Nancy's face. "I'm so sorry for keeping this from you. Will you forgive me?"

"Yes, I forgive you," says Raina.

Frank then asks, "Can you forgive us?"

She gazes at both of her parents and smiles. "Yes, I forgive the both of you. I love all of you so much."

Frank grins. "Thank you, Lord, for this day of joy you've given my sister and her daughter."

As the months go by, Raina and Nancy are inseparable.

After school activities, Raina comes home and spends time with her mother. Raina tells her everything about school, school activities, and her friends. During these months of Raina's senior year, Nancy feels and looks better than she did after the tragic event. Nancy still won't leave the house; all of her friends, family, and her psychiatrist come to the house and persuade her to go out, but to no avail.

Nancy tells Frank and Jacqueline that she never wants to go into that house again. She tells Frank to sell the house. Frank tries convincing Nancy not to sell, but she is not budging on her decision. Frank puts the house on the market for Nancy, and after a few weeks, it sells.

Frank, Jacqueline, Raina, Dora, and a couple of movers pack up and move all the furniture in the house that wasn't given to family and friends.

Raina is in Nancy's bedroom alone, packing up the remaining items out of the closet. Standing on a small step stool, she sees a black cloche hat sitting on top of a black box in the back corner of the shelf. Raina has to stand on the tip of her toes to reach and get the hat and box down. She gets down off the step stool and walks over to the vanity, places the box with the hat on the desk top, and sits down. Raina looks at the hat and places it on her head. She looks at herself in the mirror and smiles. The hat curls down around her cheek, framing her face, and it's comfortable with a soft fabric. She hums appreciatively. She looks good.

She looks down at the box before opening it slowly. There are pictures of Nancy with different family members Raina knows and doesn't know, high school pictures, and nursing school pictures with various classmates. Raina looks exactly like her in those pictures. In some, Nancy is around the same age as Raina.

Out of the many now-scattered memories, Raina picks up

one of a slim, tall, very well-dressed, and handsome man. He looks to be in his early twenties.

Raina moves a few more of the pictures and finds there is something wrapped in a white cloth. Unfolding the material, she reveals a small handgun and some type of knife in a dragon-patterned leather case. She takes the gun out of the cloth and holds it in her hand. The gun is small and nickel-plated with a brown wooden handgrip. It's a two-shot .41 caliber derringer pistol.

She studies the gun, opening the barrel to see that no bullets are in it. Frank owns guns, so Raina knows how to load and shoot rifles, as well as pistols. She looks back in the box and finds a container of bullets. She puts the gun and the knife back in the black box and places it out of the way to take home.

Nancy didn't want anything out of her old house. The remaining items—furniture, appliances, wall pictures, and art—will be donated to their local church and to the less fortunate.

Once the house is empty, Raina tells Frank and Jacqueline that she will lock up the house as she leaves. She just wants to hang back for a few minutes. Frank agrees and he, Jacqueline, and Dora drive off.

Raina walks in and out of different rooms, thinking about the good memories over the years. She admires the high ceilings, oak rail molding, beautiful hardwood floors, and large brick fireplace with a wooden mantel where Nancy's portrait had hung. Raina walks around the yard, smiling as she thought of times had there and tears running down her face at others.

Raina walks through the living room, reaching the front door. She turns around, takes one last look, and says, "I'm going to miss this house." Outside, she starts her car, looking up at the house for a moment, before driving away.

Once Raina arrives home, she picks up the boxes of items she had gathered at Nancy's house and places them on her desk upstairs. She sits down and opens up the black box, taking the knife out before placing the derringer pistol and bullets, along with the gentleman's photograph, next to it.

She thinks about the events that have happened over the past months. Raina tilts the gun around in her hands, feeling each groove and cool metallic piece beneath her fingers. She swings open the chamber and sees the ring of empty wells for the bullets.

She stands up with the pistol in her hand and faces the dresser mirror with her arms extended forward in firing position. She looks at herself holding the gun with her mother's black hat on.

She lets the gun fall to her side and walks back over to the desk. She wraps the gun in the white cloth and places it back into the box. She then picks up the dragon-patterned case and pulls the knife out. She admires the white steel, its razor-sharp blade, and the ebony handle.

She wonders what kind of knife it is, so she visits the family library, grabbing the 'K' encyclopedia, and flips through the pages until she finds the knife section. Raina turns the pages, searching through different pictures. She frowns when she can't find it, but finds another one similar that slices fish.

Once she finishes, she returns to her room. This knife is beautiful, Raina thinks, and was probably expensive. She's never seen anything like it before, but she assumes it's for cleanly cutting raw fish. She's not sure why her mother would have one, but she's certain she's never seen her with it. Regardless, she places the knife in the box, along with the derringer pistol and the box of bullets. She slides the box under her bed. She takes the picture of the guy with the red hair and places it up against a recent picture of herself she had sitting on her desk. She wonders who this guy is.

———

Early on a Saturday morning, Nancy is sitting out on the back porch, watching the sun rise up over the pine trees, when Raina sits next to her.

"Good morning, Mama."

"Good morning, baby," greets Nancy.

"Mama, I found a black box in the back of your closet when we were packing up the house. The box had a knife and a small gun. Where did you get those items from?" asks Raina.

Nancy responds, "The knife was given to me from one of my nurses I had trained with named Keiko. Keiko worked at the hospital for a few months, but went back to Japan due to the discrimination. Keiko was a wonderful girl. People mocked her because she was Japanese." She shifts and avoids Raina's gaze. "As for the gun, it belonged to…" Nancy hesitates for a moment, now looking into Raina's eyes, and says, "Francis… your father."

Nancy looks down at her cup of coffee for a moment, deciding if she should go on with what she was about to say. "Your father was a federal agent," she confesses. "The agency turned its back on him. He left his gun with me. I don't know why, but I kept it." Nancy gives Raina a stern look and continues, "Keep those items and use them if anyone ever tries to hurt you like me."

———

On Saturday evening, Alexander drives over to Raina's house to pick her up. He's taking her to his home to spend the evening. He lives with his parents while attending college and working.

It's a very nice, cool Saturday evening when he knocks on the door. Nancy answers and says through the screen door,

"Hello, Alexander. How are you?" She opens the screen door and lets him enter the house.

As Alexander walks into the house, he replies, "I'm doing well, Miss Nancy. How are you feeling this fine evening?"

"I'm doing well today," Nancy answers. "Have a seat here in the living room, Alexander. Raina just got home from the tennis courts and is upstairs taking a bath. She'll be down in a few minutes."

"I'm doing some baking with Miss Dora in the kitchen right now," she continues, "but next time you come by, let's talk, okay?"

"Yes, Miss Nancy, I'm looking forward to it!"

"You and Raina have a great evening, and tell your parents I said hello," says Nancy as she leaves the room.

"I will tell them, thanks."

About five minutes later, Raina comes down the stairs wearing a light burgundy dirndl skirt, a white blouse with a light burgundy design, and black shoes. Her head dons a light burgundy cloche hat trimmed in black with a small bow. Raina's look is magnified by her long, red hair and her flawless makeup.

Alexander stands up from the couch.

"Hello, Alexander, how are you?" Raina asks with a big, bright, beautiful smile.

"I—I'm…doing well," Alexander answers, barely getting the words out of him mouth because of Raina's magnificence. "Raina, you are beautiful."

"Thank you." She beams with a blush. "I'm ready to go if you are."

"Let's go," says Alexander as Raina settles her hand into the crook of his elbow.

The two arrive at Alexander's house. They walk into the house, entering into the family room to see Alexander's parents sitting.

"Hello, Mr. and Mrs. Mitchell," Raina greets.

They grin upon seeing her. "Raina, it's good to see you. You are so lovely, and you dress so classy," says Mrs. Mitchell.

"Thank you, Mrs. Mitchell."

The young couple sits down on the couch in the family room.

Mr. Mitchell asks, "How are your studies going?"

"I'm doing well. I have an A average, and I'm captain of the tennis team."

"How are your parents doing?"

"They are doing well. My mother is writing a book, and my father's law practice is growing. He's employing a couple more attorneys to his staff."

"Have you entertained the thought of practicing law?"

Raina laughs. "My father asks me all the time if I want to be in law, and I keep telling him no. I do help from time to time at the office, though. I want to be a nurse. Helping sick people, I feel, is my calling."

The four of them talk for about an hour before Mrs. Mitchell says to her husband, "Let's go into another room and let the kids have some time together."

The two sit in the family room with the radio on, talking about family, friends, school activities, and their developing relationship.

"Raina," Alexander starts, "I'm so fortunate to have you as my girlfriend. I love the way you laugh and the smell of your hair. You are a very good tennis player with that powerful forehand shot. You always get better test scores because you work so hard to study, and everyone likes you. You're so beautiful. I'm glad I got up the nerve to talk to you, Raina. I'm glad I met you." He moves over closer to her.

She blushes and bites her lip, attempting to stop the massive grin that's threatening to overtake her face. She brushes a piece of hair behind her ear and shyly meets his gaze. "And you're the sweetest guy I've ever met. Ever since you helped me grab my books when I dropped them in the hall, I knew."

"Thank you."

He gets close to Raina, and as they are looking into each other's eyes, Alexander's lips touch Raina's. They kiss softly, then they deepen the kiss. As they are softly yet passionately kissing, Raina timidly pushes Alexander away.

"Everything okay?" he asks.

"Everything is perfect, Alexander."

He looks at her intensely and says to Raina for the first time face-to-face, "I love you."

Raina blushes, puts her arms around him, and whispers into his ear, "I love you, too."

The next day, Frank, Jacqueline, Nancy, and Raina get up early in the morning to eat Dora's Sunday breakfast. They all get dressed for church, except for Nancy, who is still struggling to go out in public.

As Frank pulls into the church parking lot, Raina notices Concepción standing with two other girls in front of the church having casual conversation.

Raina gets out of the car and walks over to the girls. "Good morning!"

And they reply, "Good morning, Raina."

"I'm looking forward to singing this morning," says Concepción.

"Me, too. I think we had a pretty good rehearsal on Wednesday," Raina agrees.

"You have a very pretty dress on, Raina, and your hat is

fabulous," says Rachel, one of the girls in the youth choir.

"Thank you, Rachel."

Upon arriving, the youth choir director, Mrs. Kelly, says, "Everyone in the youth choir, come in, please. It's time to go to the choir stand."

"Yes, ma'am," the girls answer as the other youth choir members head to the choir room to put on their robes and get into the choir stand before church service begins.

All the youth choir members arrive to the choir stand. Mrs. Kelly plays a hymn, and the deacons start the order of service. Once the hymn ends, one of the deacons reads a Bible scripture, then another deacon leads everyone in prayer. Once prayer is over, the deacons lead the congregation in another very motivating hymn. As the devotion part of the service ends and the morning worship service begins, Senior Pastor Doyle enters the pulpit with the other three church elders. He steps to the podium while the spirit is moving in the sanctuary and says, "There has to be at least twenty-five people here that can stand up and thank God for being good to them." And many of the church attendees stand to clap and thank God for His grace and mercy.

Later in the service, the youth choir stands up to sing, "He Made a Difference in My Life." Raina starts softly, a smooth melody that melds with the organ behind her, until the chorus begins and her voice overtakes the instrument, her lasting lyrics echoing throughout the church.

Once the song is over, the congregation applauds. Before leaving, Raina, Jacqueline, and Frank spend time fellowshipping with friends at the church. Raina receives a big hug from Pastor Doyle who she really admires.

The three make their way to the car and head home. As Frank is driving, he says, "What a powerful church service today. Raina, you really did a wonderful job singing that song. I was touched."

Jacqueline says, "I agree! I really enjoyed that song, and you sang it so well."

"Thanks, Mother and Dad. I'm so glad you both enjoyed it," Raina says, grinning from ear to ear.

"Through it all, God has blessed this family so much. He is so worthy to be praised," says Frank.

Jacqueline says, "Amen."

When the Willoughby's arrive at the supermarket, Frank and Raina separate from Jacqueline to grab the produce while she handles the other end of the store.

As the two walk down the store isle to join Jacqueline, Mr. Howard, the father of Raina's friend Inell, turns back around from looking at the back of Jacqueline with a lustful look and a shake of his head.

The three meet in the isle, and Mr. Howard asks, "How are you doing, Mr. Willoughby and Miss Raina?"

"We are doing fine," Frank says in a dry voice. Everyone knows he's a womanizer.

Mr. Howard smiles. "I just spoke to your wife. What a *dish*, isn't she?"

Instantly, an enraged and disbelieving look comes over Frank's face. He can't believe Mr. Howard said that in front of Raina and him. "Mr. Howard, first of all, that's my wife you are lusting over, and second of all, that was very disrespectful to say in front of me and my daughter."

"I'm sorry, Mr. Willoughby and Miss Raina, please forgive me," he says with a half-hearted laugh, not really meaning what he just said.

"Let me give you a bit of advice. That smart mouth and flirting is going to get you a beating someday." Frank just glares at him then continues, "Have a nice day."

As he and Raina walk down the aisle to join Jacqueline, Raina realizes she's never seen her dad so mad. She's never liked Mr. Howard. Not only do the kids always tease her friend Inell about her Casanova father, but the entire Willoughby family has fallen prey to his wandering eye before.

Chapter V

I NEED YOU

THE MONTHS GO BY, AND IT IS TIME FOR RAINA to graduate from high school. She already has been accepted to attend Hillman Hospital School of Nursing.

She is sitting outside on the front porch swing with Nancy. "Aunt Nancy, I'm looking forward to graduating next week. I want you to be there. Will you come?"

"I want to, baby, and I'm going to try." Nancy sits there, silent for a moment, thinking of how to say more. "Raina, I know it's been over a year since the incident happened, but I can't get over it. I am so scared to leave the house. I want to go with my daughter shopping, to see her tennis matches and school functions, but the thought of a man or anyone else looking at me scares me so much. I start getting so nervous, my legs go numb, and my heart starts beating fast." Tears run down her face.

Raina reaches over and puts her arm around her as she leans over and lays her head on Nancy's shoulder. "Momma, don't worry about it. I understand. I love you so much."

Nancy gives a smile. Her daughter called her Momma.

With Nancy still huddled in her arms, Raina looks out to the front yard. Why did this have to happen to her mother? Her grip tightens on Nancy's shoulder. Someday, James Posey will pay for this. Someday.

———

Frank comes home from a usual day at the office. As he enters the family room, he says, "Good evening." He walks over to Jacqueline as she writes a letter and kisses her on the cheek. He gives Raina, who is sitting on the couch reading a book, the same treatment.

Taking a moment in his chair that he's plopped down in, a deep inhale fills his lungs before he sighs, catching the attention of the women in the room. He doesn't give them time to be concerned because he leans forward in his chair and says, "I received a letter from Boston on the status of James Posey. James Posey finished six months at the mental hospital. The doctor that was assigned to James's case gave the director of the hospital a report that stated James was psychologically fit to be released from the hospital with minimal restrictions. Attorney Murphy, who is also licensed to practice law in the state of Massachusetts, filed a motion to the judge, asking for his release from the hospital, which he granted. The judge also reduced James's sentence to one year probation, counting time in the hospital as served time due to good behavior. He's also allowing James's medical license to be reinstated in the state of Massachusetts once he completes his probation, providing he stays out of trouble."

There's a moment of silence before Jacqueline slams her pen down on the table. "I don't believe what I'm hearing. This madman assaulted my sister-in-law, assaulted Raina, and this is considered justice? I don't understand, Frank. How is that animal able to get away with this?"

Frank replies, "I understand you're upset, and I am also.

I'm working on getting a stay on the judge's decision. Mr. Posey has a lot of power in Boston. He has deep pockets and a lot of political strings he can pull there."

Raina says, "Dad, I know you're doing all you can. James Posey is a very bad person. It's hard to believe that people with power would manipulate the system for money or favor to keep a bad person out of jail. I just know deep in my heart that he will pay for hurting my mother and others."

Jacqueline looks at Raina, thinking how mature she has become. She should be upset and mad but has an attitude of knowing justice will prevail. Raina continues, "Thank you so much, Dad, for including me in this conversation.

She stands up from the couch and hugs Frank then Jacqueline. "I'm going to talk with Momma for a few minutes and do my homework."

"Don't mention this to Nancy," says Frank.

"Yes, sir," Raina replies as she turns and walks out of the room.

Jacqueline looks over at Frank and comments, "She is taking this very well."

"Yes," replies Frank as he stares down the hallway his daughter just retreated down. "Too well."

———

After completing her homework, Raina takes a bath and puts on her night gown. She realizes it's early, so when she finishes brushing her hair, she walks out of her room and moves across the hall to Nancy's bedroom. Raina softly knocks on the door.

"Come in," says Nancy.

Raina walks in. "How are you, Momma?"

Nancy is sitting at her vanity, brushing her black, shoulder-length hair. She smiles at Raina through the vanity mirror. "I'm doing well, my pretty daughter."

Raina stands behind Nancy and asks, "May I?" Raina gestures to the hair brush.

"Sure."

Raina begins slowly brushing her hair. Nancy is looking at herself in the mirror then asks Raina with a smile on her face, "Do you think I'm pretty?"

"Yes."

"Do you like the fragrance of my perfume?"

"Yes, why do you ask?"

"Well, back when I was younger, I would ask the young gentlemen who wanted to court me those two questions. They all said 'yes' to both, but when I waited to hear why they thought so, they never continued, so I would not entertain their company. But there was one handsome, slim, red-headed, kind, and considerate man who answered. I was more beautiful than the Mona Lisa, he said, and the scent of my perfume was like an irresistible, beautiful bouquet of flowers."

Nancy's pale face brightens with the contented smile that rests on her lips. She closes her eyes and says, "The both of us started seeing each other after that. He would always make me feel like a lady, like nothing else mattered to him in the world but me." As Nancy talks, Raina just keeps slowly brushing her hair. "I will never forget our time together. We weren't together long, then I never saw him again. I never saw Francis again, but he gave me the most beautiful gift of all."

Nancy then blinks her eyes, coming out of her deep thoughts, as if awakening from a wonderful dream. She looks up at Raina and says, "Well, I'm a little tired, and you have school in the morning, so I'm going to get in bed." She stands up and gives Raina a hug. Nancy walks over and gets into bed.

Raina places the hair brush on the vanity desk and walks

over to the door. She turns around and says, "Goodnight, Momma. I love you."

"I love you, too, my beautiful daughter."

"Thanks, Momma." Raina smiles, a blush on her cheeks, and slowly shuts the door.

Once in her room, Raina pulls the picture of herself off the vanity mirror frame. Tucked behind is the picture of the red-headed young man. She looks at the picture for a moment. So, this is her father? Raina looks down from the picture and into the vanity mirror. She looks at herself a moment, then she puts the picture back in the mirror frame behind hers and says her prayers before bed.

The next day at school, Raina is having lunch with Concepción and Inell in the cafeteria.

"I'm ready for graduation. I get to go off to college and live however I want to," says Inell with excitement. "Concepción, what are your plans?"

"I was accepted to the University of Alabama!"

"Good for you, Concepción. What will you major in?"

"Chemistry," she says, as she takes a bite of her lunch.

"What about you, Raina? What are your plans?" asks Inell.

"I'm going to attend Hillman School of Nursing."

"That's great!" Inell chirps. "We only have three weeks before graduation, and we'll be entering into the next chapter of our lives. I'm going to miss both of you next fall."

A moment later, two of the girls' classmates, Virginia and Chantel, come over to the table and sit down with their lunch trays. The newcomers' greetings are falsely chipper, but the trio's are lackluster at best.

Chantel addresses Inell pointedly, "I saw your father downtown on Saturday. Who was that woman he was with?"

"I don't know. He probably was meeting a client down there.

He does some business on the weekends because of his clients' work schedules," replies Inell.

"Does he put his arms around all his female clients?"

Concepción glares at Chantel. "Don't start, Chantel!"

Virginia pipes in, "Let's talk about something else, girls."

Chantel carries on. "I want to talk about Mr. Howard. He has so many lady clients from what I hear. He can't seem to keep his hands off of them."

"Chantel," Concepción snaps, "you need to cut it out! You are always starting a mess."

Chantel moves her lunch tray over to the side and leans slightly forward, ignoring Concepción. "I'm pissed off! I was at the grocery store last week, Inell, when your father came up to me, asking me how I was doing and if I needed anything, I could come over and see him personally at his office. He couldn't resist putting his hands on me!"

Raina says, "You really need to shut up now."

Concepción followed by saying, "Girls, let's stop the arguing."

Chantel, who is now very mad, looks over at Raina with a fiery glow, her face as red as a cherry. "You don't need to say anything, you arrogant ass!" she growls. "You really make me sick! You and that red hair, you have to be the daughter of the devil."

Raina stands up, ready to fight, and yells, "Shut up, Chantel, before I punch you in the face!"

The loud outburst silences the lunch room, and one of the teachers gets up from the table she is eating lunch at and walks over to the girls' table, asking, "Is there a problem here?"

Raina continues to scowl at Chantel, but says after a moment, "No problem, Miss Rutledge. Just acting out a scene from our drama class." Raina slowly sits back down.

Miss Rutledge warns, "Keep it down."

As Miss Rutledge turns and leaves the table, tears run down

Inell's face. She gets up and runs out of the lunch room.

Raina follows close behind. "Inell," shouts Raina as she catches up with her, quickly walking down the hallway and placing her hand on Inell's shoulder. The two sit down on the bench in the hallway.

"Inell, don't let Chantel get you upset. She can be a fathead at times just because her dad is the mayor," says Raina as she puts an arm around her shoulders. "Chantel is just jealous of you. You're athletic, smart, and the prettiest girl in school." She winks. "Second to me, of course."

Inell laughs, and Raina continues, "In a couple of weeks, you and I won't have to see Chantel again. Now, let's go get our books and go to the gym. Let's go watch the boys!"

Inell wipes the last tear from her face and laughs some more. Raina grabs Inell's hand, and the both of them stand up and head to their lockers.

———

That Friday night, Raina packs a bag and drives to Concepción's house for a sleepover.

Once the girls are dressed for bed, they sit on Concepción's bed against the head board, pillows cushioned against their backs.

"Concepción," Raina starts, "I have something I want to tell you."

Concepción pauses in combing her doll's hair and glances at Raina. "What is it?"

"This is important," Raina stresses.

Concepción puts her doll down on the side of the bed and puts her hand on Raina's. "Okay, tell me what's on your mind."

"You know my Aunt Nancy and I have a lot in common. We like cooking, sewing, reading, and dressing nice. And, of course, we love our hats and perfume." Raina pauses for a moment, looking down.

"What is it, Raina?"

Raina raises her head up to look at her best friend and says, "Nancy is my biological mother."

"What?"

"You heard me right. Nancy is my mother," Raina says as she looks back down at the doll. The room is quiet. Concepción is analyzing what she just heard.

"Raina, tell me, why you are just now finding this out?" asks Concepción.

"Aunt Nancy got pregnant by a guy she really loved, but she was only fifteen years old. My grandparents were very upset about her pregnancy, so they sent her to Alden where she lived with our Aunt Louise to birth me."

Concepción is looking at Raina with confusion. "How did you end up living with your parents? I mean, your uncle and aunt, right?"

She nods and explains calmly. "My father didn't want me separated from Nancy, so he and my mother made the decision to ask Aunt Nancy if they could raise me. They asked her to move in with them and finish school there so she could be in my life. They decided later on they would tell me the truth when I was ready. The assault made them decide it was time."

"Wow! That is really surprising, but it makes sense. You and Nancy look a lot alike: your body types, eyes, facial structure. If you dyed your hair black, you two would almost be identical twins.

"So how do you address two mothers by name?"

"I still call Frank 'Dad' and Jacqueline 'Mother,' but I now call Nancy 'Momma.'" Raina giggles. Concepción grins and lunges at Raina for big hug. "I love you, sis!"

Chapter VI

TOMORROW

❦ **T**HE DAY HAS ARRIVED: Raina's high school graduation."
Jacqueline proudly beams while sitting at the breakfast
table with Frank, Nancy, and Raina.

"It seems like yesterday that I was changing your diapers
and feeding you baby food," says Dora as she takes up the finished breakfast plates from the table.

"She has grown to become a very fine young lady," Frank
agrees as he looks at Raina proudly.

Nancy says, "Yes, Frank, she is a very intelligent and talented young lady, and I'm so proud of my daughter."

"Thanks, everyone. I'm really glad you all are proud of me.
I want everyone to know that I'm so thankful for my family.
This family has shown me so much love and support." Raina
gets up from the table and hugs Dora as she puts the dishes in
the sink and gives her a kiss on the cheek. She then bends down
to hug and kiss Frank, Jacqueline, then Nancy, lingering on the
last to tell her, "I love you." She sits back down and addresses
her again. "Momma, are you going to come to my graduation
this evening?"

Nancy looks unsure and replies, "I don't know, baby."

Frank takes the focus away from his sister, saying assuredly,

"We will be taking lots of pictures." He gets up from the table. "I'm going to get a couple of things from the store on my way to work." Frank kisses Jacqueline and says, "See you all this evening!"

Jacqueline gets up after her husband. "I'm headed to work, as well. Everyone have a good day!" she calls as she gets her satchel.

Raina leaves for the day as well, with one last heartfelt good-bye from Nancy before she drives off to her last day of high school.

Nancy knows she needs to think about Raina's graduation, but that's what she's enjoyed about her newfound routine of cleaning with Dora and helping Jacqueline with her work—not thinking. She doesn't linger on the past when she has tasks to complete.

—

Raina arrives at school to a very lax day. Students are in classes, but they are conversing and playing games such as chess, checkers, and cards.

It's announced that graduation practice will begin after lunch and seniors will be dismissed afterwards.

"I'm so excited about the ceremony!" Concepción cheers.

"Excited?" Inell scoffs. "I'm terrified! I just know I'm going to trip on my way up!"

Raina laughs. "I'm sure we'll all do fine."

Rachel says, "This will be the next chapter of our lives. After tonight, we won't see each other every day. We're going our separate ways."

"It's been a fun four years together with you, Rachel," says Inell. "I remember the first thing I said to you was, 'where are you from?' You moving here from England, I couldn't understand your European accent," says Inell.

"Inell, when I met you four years ago, I knew we would hit it off. You are a wonderful, caring person who I have grown to love," says Concepción with a sentimental expression on her face.

"Susan, you have always been the level-headed one in our class. That's probably why you're our class president. You are the nicest person I have ever met," says Inell.

Raina stands up. "I love all you girls and will miss seeing you every day." The rest stand, and each join in for a group hug.

———

Frank arrives at the office.

"Good morning, Mr. Willoughby," his personal office secretary, Deloris, says.

"Good morning, Deloris! How's everything going?"

"Everything is good. I made sure you don't have any meetings today," she quickly informs, then turns to him with a smile as he sets his briefcase down in his office. "So, how's Raina doing today? I'm sure she's excited about graduating."

As Frank stands in his office doorway, he says, "I was a little disappointed to hear she didn't want to follow in my footsteps, but I'm still happy she's choosing to be something that will make her happy."

"That's great, Mr. Willoughby! Will she be interning here at the office this summer?"

As Frank sits down in one of the chairs in front of Deloris's desk, he replies, "Yes, she will be here helping us out. I've been trying to get her into law, but she is standing firm that she wants to be a nurse. I have to say, she's a very focused young adult who knows what she wants and doesn't let anything stop her when her mind is made up."

"It's good to hear a kid her age knows what she wants. She is mature and has wisdom beyond her young years. Everyone here at the office will be at the graduation tonight."

Grinning, Frank replies, "Great! We are expecting a large crowd of family and friends to be at the graduation and over to the house tonight. My little girl is a young lady now. She has her whole life ahead of her."

———

"Good morning, Mrs. Willoughby! I bet Raina is excited about graduating from high school today," Geneva, one of the deputy editors, says as she passes by Mrs. Willoughby's desk. "I'm very excited about Elmer graduating today. I never thought this day would come." Geneva has a joyous look on her face as she hands Mrs. Willoughby her typed letters that need approval. "It was always a shame that Elmer and Raina never really got along. I actually hoped they would go on a few dates!" She sends Jacqueline a teasing grin. "That way, we could giggle and tease them over their awkward dating years."

"We're having a graduation party for Raina tonight. You and your family are welcome to attend. I'm sorry for the short notice, Geneva, but we just decided to do this at the last minute," says Jacqueline.

"Thank you for the invitation. Ralph and I may come by for a little while, but Elmer wants to hang out with his friends after the ceremony. We have a card for Raina, though, we'll give to her after the ceremony is over."

"I'm sure she'll love it." She smiles. "Has Elmer decided what he wants to do next?"

"Not completely. He doesn't want to go to college, so we think he wants to join the military." Her mouth pulls into a worried frown.

"Well, I understand you don't want him to join the military, but he has to make his own decisions now."

"I know, but I want him to go to college. Like you said, though, it's his decision, it's his life," Geneva says with a sigh.

"The good thing is you and Ralph have done a great job raising him to make the right decisions moving forward in the next chapter of his life."

"Thank you. We have two wonderful kids graduating from high school tonight."

Jacqueline smiles brightly. "Yes, we do, Geneva. Yes, we do!"

Chapter VII

BREAK EVERY CHAIN

I
T'S AROUND TWO O'CLOCK THAT AFTERNOON when Nancy
walks into the kitchen after hanging some graduation decorations for the party.

"Dora, how did the cake turn out?" Nancy asks.

"Give me a few minutes more," Dora says as she squirts a
little more red frosting over the top of the cake, "and the cake'll
be all finished."

Nancy stands at the kitchen table in awe, looking at the
cake covered in white icing with a waving, red rope design. The
three-level sheet cake has the shape of a graduation cap on top
in red. The cake looks like it was sculpted.

"It looks amazing, Dora!" Nancy gushes.

"Thank you, Miss Nancy." She puts the blue icing in a small
bag to start the writing.

"Dora, can I talk to you about something?" Nancy asks after
a few moments.

Dora looks over the top of her reading glasses, pausing her
piping. "Yes, Miss Nancy, we can talk."

"Let's sit down," Nancy says. Dora sits down at the head of
the kitchen table with Nancy to her left.

Jill, one of the maids from the neighbor's house, is helping

Dora bake and decorate for the party. "Jill, can you go into the dining room and polish the table?" asks Dora.

"Yes, Dora." Jill leaves the kitchen, and Dora turns back to Nancy. She asks, "What's on your mind, Miss Nancy?"

"Dora, I want to go to Raina's graduation so badly, but I'm scared." Her voice hitches, and she wrings her hands together. "She wants her mother there, but I'm scared to leave the house."

Dora lays a cautious hand on her shoulder. "Miss Nancy," she starts softly and hesitantly. Any time they'd try to talk to the woman, she usually brushed them off and walked away in a panicked hurry. "Are you scared of the way people may look at you? What they may say about you?"

Nancy looks down at the kitchen table and answers, "Yes, I don't want to be looked at as the lady that was beaten. I think about them saying such awful things. I did nothing to cause this, Dora. I didn't do anything. I didn't deserve what happened to me. I'm so scared, Dora. I'm scared!" Tears run down her face.

"You're absolutely right. You did nothing wrong, but you can't control what people say or think." Dora shifts in her chair and changes her tone. "Look up at me, Miss Nancy." She looks Nancy right in her eyes, saying, "Miss Nancy, you have a strong, smart, and very beautiful daughter who needs the old Nancy. The Nancy who is independent, strong, successful, and very beautiful inside and out. Your daughter needs you, Miss Nancy. God did not create us to fear anything or anyone. It's time to live life again, Miss Nancy, not fear it! Don't you miss your life? Don't you?!"

"Yes, Dora, I do miss it."

"Well, do something about it, and the time is now! If you don't do it for yourself, do it for Raina, *your daughter*," Dora finishes in a stern voice that Nancy had never heard before, a voice that stirs something inside of Nancy, a flame in her spirit.

"You have to put on one of your fine dresses, your makeup, and a pretty hat for your daughter's graduation. You need to do it for her and yourself," she continues, looking over the top of her reading glasses again. "Baby, it's time to hold your head up, pull your shoulders back, and move forward. It's time to get your life back, Miss Nancy!"

Nancy gets up from the seat at the table and heads to her room with a look of determination.

———

Raina walks into the house around one o'clock to find her parents and Dora gathered around an artfully decorated living room.

"Wow!" Raina exclaims as she looks around the living room. There are lots of balloons, pictures of Raina through-out the years, and a big sign hanging over the fireplace mantel, saying, "Congratulations, Raina." Her letterman sweater and tennis rackets lay out on a table with high school pictures of her. She almost hides her face in embarrassment at her first-grade drawing hanging between her numerous trophies. In her unsteady child's hand, she'd scrawled two bulbous figures that were supposed to be her and Aunt Nancy, if the bright red hair on the smaller form and the untidy "Ant Nansee" underneath the larger tells her anything.

"So, you like what you see?" Jacqueline asks as she hangs the high school mascot sign. Raina is still walking around the living room, looking at all the pictures and items from over the years that Jacqueline had collected. "Mother, the living room looks great!"

Raina walks into the dining room, and it's decorated with signs and congratulations cards. The dining room table is set up with plates and sterling serving dishes for food that will be set out later for the guests once the ceremony is over.

Raina picks up the framed first-place award for a writing competition she won in the fourth grade. She is interrupted from her memories the memorabilia brings back by her mother in the other room. "Raina, go ahead and get yourself cleaned up and dressed for the graduation!" She touches some of her old first-grade drawings and smiles before going up the stairs to her room. Raina says from the top step, "Everyone, the house looks magnificent! Thanks Mother, Father, and you too, Miss Dora."

"You're welcome," they call, still finishing up the decorations.

Raina stops at Nancy's door on the way and knocks. "Momma, are you going to come down and see me before I leave for the graduation?"

Nancy replies through the door, "I will be down in a few minutes." Raina was just about to ask Nancy if she was going to come to her graduation, but she just looks down and says, "Okay, see you in a minute, Momma." Raina turns and walks to the next door across the hall and goes into her room.

A short time later, Frank comes into the living room with his Kodak camera. Jacqueline is already dressed and downstairs with Dora, finishing the food preparation with two other maids. Frank shouts, "Come on down, Raina, so we can take some pictures. We don't want you to arrive late for your graduation."

Raina comes out of her room and stops at Nancy's bedroom door. She knocks. "Momma, we are meeting downstairs to take pictures. Come down and take some pictures with me before I leave, okay?"

"Give me a minute, and I will be down," she answers.

Raina stands at Nancy's bedroom door for a few seconds, wondering if she should ask her mother again to come to the graduation. Raina looks down at the door knob instead and whispers, "I really wish you would come, Momma." Raina raises her head, puts her fingertips on the door, and walks away downstairs into the living room. Nancy is standing against the door and heard what Raina had whispered.

"There's the young lady!" Franks says as he sees her on the steps.

Jacqueline says, "Look at you! You look so beautiful in your cap and gown."

Raina looks stunning with her cap and tassel resting on her shoulder-length hair, wearing immaculate makeup like a movie star.

"Come over here in front of the fireplace so I can get a picture of you," says Frank. The maids and Dora come out of the dining room to see Raina.

"My little Red looks wonderful. She grew up so fast," Dora gushes.

Raina stands in front of the fireplace facing Frank, who holds the camera up and says, "Say cheese!"

Just as she's about to pose for the picture, she looks up just above Frank, and her jaw drops.

"What's wrong, Raina? What are you looking at?" Frank turns around, and everyone watches as Nancy, standing there in a white dress with green flowers and a matching green waist band and handbag, descends the stairs. Her black hair falls just below the shoulders under her white cloth hat. Her makeup is flawless, and she looks like a model.

The room is so quiet. Nancy says, "Close your mouths before something flies in." She lightly laughs and walks the remaining few steps, almost as if she were modeling the dress.

Everyone in the room is in awe. Nancy looks like her old self, but with a new fire inside of her. Raina smiles at her mother so brightly she could have lit up the darkest night. Jacqueline and Frank glance at each other as if to say, "That's the Nancy we know."

"Momma, come and take a picture with me." She grabs Nancy's arm and pulls her over in front of the fireplace.

"Dora, what did you say to her?" asks Jill.

"I just said to let no one have control over your life and to get off your ass and go to your daughter's graduation." Dora laughs.

"Okay, girls, let's get close together and give me a big smile," Frank directs as he positions the camera up to his face to take the picture. The two stand next to each other with two smiles that are blindingly beautiful.

"Say cheese!" Frank snaps the picture as the bulb on the camera flashes. He lowers the camera and says, "My goodness, you two look so much alike."

Jacqueline agrees, "They could almost pass for twin sisters." She smiles at both and holds her hands against her chest, thankful to see Nancy going to the graduation.

Everyone in the room takes turns standing with Raina for pictures. Frank then puts the camera on its tripod while Nancy, Jacqueline, and Frank stand with Raina to take a group picture. Just before Frank presses the button, setting the timer, he quickly shuffles into place next to his family. Frank asks Dora to join.

"Yes, Mr. Willoughby, I would be honored," replies Dora as she takes off her apron and joins in the pose.

"Willoughby family," says Frank, "say cheese!" Everyone follows his instructions, and the camera bulb flashes.

———

Frank, Jacqueline, Nancy, and Raina arrive at the high school. Raina goes to the area where her classmates are meeting before the ceremony begins. Frank, Jacqueline, and Nancy walk out into the football stadium and begin talking and mingling with the other parents, faculty, and friends.

Many people attending the graduation greet Nancy. She's really enjoying herself, talking with everyone who passes in front of her and speaking with some of her old coworkers from the hospital. Nancy is like she was before. No, she is like new! It's like she was reborn. It's like she's making up for the many months of solitude and self-blame.

Frank and Jacqueline are walking around and speaking with other parents and faculty staff.

"Look, Frank, there's Alexander headed over this way," says Jacqueline.

As Alexander walks up to the family, he says, "Good evening, Mr. and Mrs. Willoughby." He gives Mrs. Willoughby a hug and Mr. Willoughby a handshake. "I spoke with Raina this morning. She's excited!"

"Yes, she is," Jacqueline agrees. "Are your parents here?"

"Yes, Mrs. Willoughby, they will be arriving soon. I came over straight from work."

She nods then tilts her head to the right. "Alexander, go up front and give Nancy a hug." Alexander gives a look of surprise, then one of joy. "Yes, ma'am," he says and heads up front to see Nancy.

A few minutes later, Nancy turns around and there stands Alexander. "Hi! Miss Nancy, you are looking very nice," he compliments.

She gives a big smile and says, "Thank you, Alexander. You are looking very handsome yourself."

As the graduation ceremony for the Class of 1941 begins, Frank, Jacqueline, and Nancy take seats in the fourth row behind the graduating students.

Everyone is asked to stand. The band plays "Pomp and Circumstance," then the graduating class processional enters down the center aisle to their designated seating area directly in front of the stage.

As Raina passes Frank, Jacqueline, and Nancy, she glances over at the three and gives a huge smile and slight wave. The three wave back, and Nancy has tears of joy in her eyes. Raina also sees Alexander and gives him a wave as he waves back.

As the graduates take their place standing in front of their seats, the music subsides. One of the teachers conducts the national anthem. The school principal gives the opening remarks.

Concepción, the salutatorian, walks up on the stage and stands in front of the podium. She locks eyes with Raina and winks before starting the welcoming address. Raina winks back and nods. Her address is excellent, and everyone stands and applauds.

Shortly after, the staff distributes certificates. As the graduates' names are called, each one crosses the stage, receiving their diplomas and ovations from friends and families. As Raina's name is called, she crosses the stage and a large applause erupts, the loudest yet. Nancy applauds and turns to shout, "That's my daughter, that's my daughter!" while Frank and Jacqueline cheer, "Good job!" They look at each other and hug. Raina spends time hugging and congratulating her classmates after the ceremony ends. Concepción approaches her best friend and says, "Congratulations, sis!" They give each other a big hug.

"Thanks! I'll see you at the house later, right?"

"Yes!" The two then hug and talk to other classmates. Minutes afterwards, Raina joins Nancy and gives her a big hug.

"Congratulations, baby!" Nancy says with tears running down her face.

"Thank you, Momma. I'm so glad you came to my graduation."

"I would not have missed it for the world."

Frank and Jacqueline walk up to Raina for their hugs. Frank grins at her. "Congratulations! I'm so proud of you!"

"Thank you!" Tears gather in her eyes, too. Raina then gives Jacqueline a big hug, "Congratulations, Raina! You have made all of us so proud of you. Truly, you are a blessing to our family."

Raina wipes away the tears. "Thank you so much, Mother. I am so fortunate to have two of the best mothers in the world." She grins.

Nancy sidles up next to her daughter and says, "Raina, give me your tassel off your cap." Raina unwinds the tassel and gives it to Nancy. "Now, go and talk with your classmates. We're going to speak with some of the parents. We'll meet you at the refreshments area."

Just before Raina can say a word, Alexander walks up, and Raina jumps into his arms, kissing him on the lips.

"Wow." He exhales when she leans back. He clears his throat and grins, astonished that she kissed him like that, especially in front of their parents. "Uh…congratulations, Raina!"

"Thank you," Raina chirps, giving a smile that's so radiant, it always stops him in his tracks. "Come on, Alexander!" She pulls him by the hand to mingle.

Alexander's parents find the Willoughby family and Mr. Mitchell greets, "Hello, Frank." The two gentlemen shake hands.

"Good to see you, George and Eileen," says Frank as he gives Eileen a hug.

Jacqueline hugs both of them. "Hello, so good to see the both of you."

"Raina sure is a big girl now, Frank. Is she going to go into law?" asks George.

"Look at this beautiful lady here! Nancy, it is so good to see you here." George takes a couple of steps over and gives her a hug. Eileen steps over and gives her a hug also, excited to see her.

"It's good to be here to see my daughter graduate," says Nancy.

Eileen blinks. "You have a daughter?"

Nancy smiles. "Yes. Raina."

Eileen looks at Nancy then looks at Jacqueline. She is speechless.

Jacqueline says, "Let the three of us take a walk so we can explain."

"Okay." Eileen nods. Frank and George converse about business while the three ladies walk toward the refreshments area. Explaining to Eileen that Nancy is Raina's biological mother is the beginning of what many people will know: the secret is no more.

Alexander arrives at the house with Raina and a few of their friends trailing behind. Raina stayed behind at school to finish saying goodbye while the rest of her family went ahead to prepare for guests.

Raina and Alexander talk and laugh on the hood of his car as they wait for her classmates to catch up to go into the house together.

"Come on, you bums! Let's go, I'm hungry." Raina laughs. She and Alexander walk up to the porch, where Raina is greeted by family members and friends. She's congratulated and hugged again.

"Thank you, everyone!" Raina says as she makes her way into the house. Nancy is there, greeting people.

She sees Raina and announces in a loud, excited voice as she extends her arms out openly, "Everyone, the Willoughby's Class of 1941 graduate, and my daughter, Raina Willoughby!"

Everyone in the living room applauds, though some relatives

and friends look puzzled by Nancy's comment. Raina hugs her mother.

Leaving Raina to greet the guests, Alexander takes a cold bottle of Buffalo Rock ginger ale out of the ice cooler and takes a sip.

Raina's father enters the room. "Alexander, how's school and work going?"

"All is well with both. I'm thinking about changing my major from accounting to business law, though," he says with a pointed smile.

Frank laughs and sips his beer. "A man after my own heart. That would be a great idea with the city growing leaps and bounds."

"Would you have an internship position at your law firm if I decide to switch?"

Frank pats him on the shoulder and says, "You're a smart kid, Alexander. I know you would make a good attorney. I think one of my partners at the firm could use a good intern. Let's go out on the porch so I can persuade you to change your major, young man." Frank puts his arm around Alexander's shoulders, and they walk out of the living room.

Meanwhile, a close friend of Jacqueline's greets her. "Hello, Jacqueline!"

"Mary!" She smiles, and they hug. "It's so good to see you."

"Good to see you too, Jacqueline. I spoke to Raina and Nancy a few minutes ago. Raina is so excited, as well as Nancy. I can't tell who's the most excited between the two." She laughs.

"Yes, I know. Those two are having a blast this evening. Is Henry here with you?"

"No, my workaholic husband is at the office. "A mayor's job is never done."

Mary says then asks, "It's so good to see Nancy back to her old self. She's looking magnificent."

"Come with me," Jacqueline requests, and they shift to an equally decorated backyard. The two ladies walk out to the far end of the yard where a cement bench sits. They have a good view of everyone outside.

"You know," Jacqueline starts, "for many months, Nancy would not leave the house after the incident, but today when we were about to take pictures with Raina before graduation, she came downstairs with an attitude we had never seen from her. Mary, she even drove back from the graduation, which is wonderful! You think this personality is here to stay?"

"I hope so." She pauses. "Jacqueline, I was surprised to hear Nancy announce Raina as her daughter. I'm sure Raina knew before today, but no one else did. How do you feel about this?"

Jacqueline stares at the ground for a few seconds then replies, "I was a little shocked for a moment, but then I realized Nancy has had to live in silence for years. As Raina grew and made accomplishments along the way, she had to watch and couldn't say, 'that's my child.' She was assaulted in her home, and she needed to let it out. This was the proudest moment for her daughter, so it was time. I'm very happy for her." A look of joy on her face.

Mary pauses a moment and shifts in her seat. "Jacqueline… I do have to ask…"

Jacqueline tilts her head. "What?"

"Does Raina know who her father is?"

Jacqueline looks out at Raina having fun, talking and laughing with the other classmates and family, then turns back to Mary. "Yes, we have told her about her father but not everything."

Mary flicks her gaze to Jacqueline then shifts her attention back over at the kids and replies, "I know we aren't supposed to talk about him, but I can still hardly believe how the agency turned their backs on him like that."

Jacqueline sighs then gestures to the laughing teens. "Look how vibrant she is, how beautiful, bold and confident, mature and wise, determined and focused. She is so young, liked, and loved by many. Raina has an unlimited potential to be whatever she wants to be in life."

Jacqueline looks back at Mary and adds, "This is not the time to tell her everything about her father. When it is time, Nancy will be the one, the only one, who needs to tell her."

Mary puts her arm around Jacqueline and says, smiling, "You raised a wonderful young lady. Great job!"

All the kids in the backyard gather around the table where Raina is sitting. Charlene and Ann, classmates who sang in the school concert choir with Raina, sit on either side of her. Charlene says, "Let's sing the school anthem together."

Ann adds, "Let's get everyone to sing."

Raina smiles and replies, "Watch this." She stood up on the table. "Everyone gather around! Let's sing our school anthem song."

Right after she speaks, Concepción steps up onto the table and says, "Come, Mighty Tigers! Let's sing!"

The four girls sing, and others join in.

"Wisdom and Virtue," our motto is clear.
We will strive to uphold it in every school year.
O let us recall it when each term arrives
so that it will serve us the rest of our lives.

Everyone in the backyard joins in for the chorus.

Rosedale School, Rosedale School!
We will follow its rule,
we will honor its name.
Bring it credit and fame.

Drawn by the singing, guests follow the noise into the backyard. Nancy is speaking with Karen, a nurse under her at the hospital and a very good friend, when they hear.

As the two walk out of the kitchen area and out onto the back deck, she sees Raina and Concepción standing on one of the picnic tables, surrounded by classmates, family, and friends—all singing.

Watching Raina, Nancy is reminded of how she was at that age.

"This is amazing," Karen says. "These kids really care about each other. And there are so many singing together!"

Nancy replies, "There has to be over seventy-five kids out here. Even your son is out there singing. He was co-captain of the football team and star baseball player, wasn't he? I know you must be a proud mother." She pats Karen's hand resting next to hers on the porch deck rail.

"Yes, I am very proud of him." Karen looks at Nancy and says, "I didn't know Raina was your daughter, though."

Nancy smiles. "Yes, she is, Karen. Yes, she is. Long story, but I will tell you about it later."

They listen to the singing.

> When school days are ended and our ways depart,
> Rosedale School's ideals will remain in our hearts.
> May we make of our country, our work, and our home
> a haven of peace in which God has His throne.
> Rosedale School, Rosedale School!
> We will follow its rule,
> we will honor its name.
> Bring it credit and fame.

After singing, everyone applauds, whistles, and chants. Then Raina starts the chant, "Go, Tigers, go!" She stomps her foot on the picnic table three times.

"Go, Tigers, go!" *Thump, thump, thump.*

Everyone joins in, and the echo is so loud, one could hear it a few streets away. After about seven times, the crowd claps again. Alexander lifts Raina then Concepción down off the table.

As the evening goes on and gets later, the crowd dwindles. Raina and her family members give hugs as they walk guests to the front, wishing them a good night. Raina hugs and kisses on the cheek most of her classmates as they leave.

Nancy walks Karen out to her car. "I'm so glad you came over with Tommy. I see he's headed out to the soda shop with the other kids."

Karen replies, "The kids are so excited. They have a lot to look forward to and so much opportunity at their age. Speaking of opportunity, are you coming back to the hospital? We need you back. Old Hag Mrs. Gray is running the place like it's a military unit." Both of them chuckle.

Nancy finally controls her laughing enough to answer, "Karen, I think it is time for me to go back. I'm going up to the hospital on Monday morning to talk about coming back."

Karen gives Nancy a hug. "Wonderful! Once I tell Dr. Davis you're coming back, the red carpet will be laid out. It's going to be great for everyone, including you. The two of us back on the floor together again; it's going to be great."

"The dynamic duo is back," says Nancy as the two hug again.

Karen whispers, "I missed you, girl."

Nancy sees Karen off and the teens that come around the corner shortly after. She makes sure to kiss Raina goodbye as they head to the malt shop. Nancy walks up on the porch and watches the kids drive away. Nancy waves and vows to get herself back in the world. She had a great day with her lovely daughter, so it's time to be a mother. Nancy smiles and walks into the house.

—

Raina and Alexander return later that night. They sit on the porch swing in the fair temperature under a starlit sky.

"How do you feel being a high school graduate?" asks Alexander as he picks up Raina's hand to hold it.

She shrugs. "I don't feel any different right now, but I'm sure in a couple of weeks the reality will set in that I'm no longer in high school. I'm a young adult."

"Raina, I'll be starting my sophomore year in college this coming fall, and you will be starting nursing school. We'll both finish school around the same time," remarks Alexander.

"You're right. What are you thinking?"

"Well, we have a very good relationship, and I love you. I hope to marry you someday," he says softly.

Raina blushes. "Alexander, that is so sweet. I know you care about me. I care a lot about you, too. Let's finish school first, then we can talk about it, okay?"

Alexander smiles and says, "Okay."

Raina bumps his shoulder with hers. "I had a wonderful day. I graduated from high school, my family gave a terrific graduation party, I had a ton of fun with my friends, and shared it with my boyfriend, but," she says as she stands up, "I think it's time for me to go in."

Alexander stands and faces her. "I had terrific time with you today, and congratulations again."

Raina winds her arms around his neck as he puts his hands around her waist. Alexander says, "I really enjoyed sharing this special day with you. I love you, Raina."

She leans forward and puts her lips against his. After a minute, Raina slowly pulls her lips away and lays her head on Alexander's shoulder as he holds her close. Raina then says, "Thank you, Alexander, for being here with me."

———

Due to the impending war for the United States, the vast majority of the population is just nervously watching the Axis powers encroaching on the world. A week after Raina's high school graduation, Alexander is drafted into the Marine Corps. Raina, along with his family and friends, are at the bus station downtown to see Alexander off.

After hugs and kisses from his parents and friends, Alexander turns to Raina, leaning in to embrace her. "I'm going to miss you. I love you, Raina."

She holds on tightly to him. As tears run down her face, Raina replies, "I'm going to miss you, too. I love you! I'm going to write you every day!"

Once Raina and Alexander lean away from each other, Alexander picks up his suitcase and boards the bus, finding a seat next to the widow.

As the bus drives away, Raina waves and blows Alexander a kiss, as do the rest of his friends and family. Alexander pokes his head out of the window, waving back. "Love you all! I love you, Raina! I'll be back!"

Chapter VIII

NEVER WOULD HAVE MADE IT

Monday comes, and Nancy looks great as she walks up to the front desk on the third floor at the Hillman Hospital that a year prior she supervised.

Nancy visits with other nurses, doctors, and employees on the floor before making her way down to the administration offices.

Dr. Davis comes out of his office, almost running into Nancy, and freezes. He blinks a few times at her before a grin overtakes his face. "Nancy! Oh my God! Is that you?" He hurriedly greets her with a hug. "I'm so happy to see you. Nancy, you look great!" Dr. Davis lays his handful of files on the floor and holds both of Nancy's hands.

"I'm doing much better, Dr. Davis," she answers with a smile.

"Let's go into my office and talk." Dr. Davis picks up his files off the hallway floor and ushers her inside.

"Dr. Davis, don't you have patient checks going on?" asks Nancy.

He replies with a chuckle and a smile. "They aren't going anywhere. They can wait."

They both sit down at his desk. Dr. Davis grins. "You look great! How are you feeling? It's really good to see you here."

"I feel great, Dr. Davis. It's good to be here, seeing everyone.

I miss all of you so much."

"The floor misses you, this hospital misses you! The place is not the same without you. Nancy, you ran the third floor like no one I've ever seen. You were hands-down the best nurse and supervisor this hospital has ever had. Please tell me you're here because you want to come back."

"Yes." she nods. "I want to come to work if there's an opening. I know Mrs. Gray is now the floor supervisor, but I would take whatever opening the nursing staff has available!"

As Dr. Davis looks down then back up at Nancy, he replies, "Well, we actually have a few positions open, so you can take your pick between them, but Ms. Gray is retiring next month, and we will be needing a third-floor nurse supervisor." He smiles. "Are you interested?"

Nancy's face lights up. "Oh—oh my goodness. Yes, I'm very interested in the position! Thank you! Thank you so much!" she gushed, practically bouncing in her seat.

Dr. Davis laughs and says, "Let me walk down to the HR office and reintroduce you to Mrs. Griffin so I can make my floor rounds."

As they both stand, Dr. Davis looks at Nancy and continues, "I have a quick question. I heard that Raina is your daughter. Is that true?"

As Nancy smiles, she says, "She's my beautiful daughter."

Dr. Davis nods his head a little, waits a moment, and replies, "She is beautiful, just like her mother." He steps over and gives Nancy a hug. "Welcome back, Nancy. Welcome back."

A couple of weeks pass before Nancy returns to work. Mrs. Gray retires, and Nancy jumps into her old position as the nurse's supervisor. Soon after getting acclimated to her job duties, Nancy is promoted to the supervisor of nursing over both shifts.

She has become more confident in herself and in her abilities as a new manager and, more importantly, as a woman. She has a life again, spending time with friends, eating out with coworkers, shopping for clothes and perfumes and her favorite thing: hats. Nancy and Raina spend more time together, and Nancy is becoming the strong mother she wants to be.

Raina starts the summer working at the law firm, going through the mail, typing letters, and running errands. Even though her father is one of the law firm partners, Raina still arrives at work early and stays late at times to help get files ready for court the next day. She is always lending a helping hand to the secretary, paralegals, and partnering attorneys. The staff is always trying to convince her to go to college and become an attorney, but she always declines.

If Raina is not spending time with her family, she is with her friends at the malt shop, bowling alley, movie theater, or just hanging out. Raina writes Alexander at least three times a week while he's at Paris Island in basic training. He writes back just as much—Alexander loves her, and she loves him.

On Sunday mornings, the Willoughbys attend church, and the four are involved in different auxiliaries there. Raina is telling everyone how excited she is to start nursing school. Until recently, she's always said, "All I ever want to be is a nurse like my Aunt Nancy." Now, she says, "All I ever want to be is the best nurse in the world, like my momma."

September 1st has arrived, and what a memorable summer it was, filled with opportunities and blessings for the Willoughbys. Nancy getting her life back after the tragic incident in her home and moving forward, becoming bigger and better, is what she needed. A woman of beauty and strength has returned sociably to her friends, family, daughter, and, most importantly, herself.

Frank was promoted to senior partner at the law firm. He had spearheaded the firm to become the biggest in the state.

There are now conversations in Frank's circles of putting his hat in the ring for judgeship in the county.

Jacqueline's writings in the newspaper and columns of the local and regional magazines catapulted her to a lucrative full-time position for the city newspaper as a senior editor.

This day, Raina skips to the top of the stairs and calls to Jacqueline and Nancy down in the living room, "Good morning, everyone!"

Raina is attired in her gray, white wide-collar, and black tie student nursing uniform.

"Look at our girl! She looks great!" says Nancy.

"You look wonderful, just like your mother on her first day of nursing school," Jacqueline adds with a big smile.

She grins and glides down the remaining stairs. "Thank you, Mother and Momma."

Then Frank comes into the living room and sees Raina. "Oh my goodness! Look at my daughter." He places his hands on her shoulders and looks down at her in her uniform. "Your first day of nursing school, and you will definitely be the prettiest nurse there."

"Thank you, Father," Raina says as she receives a hug from Frank.

"Let's take some pictures, Raina. Stand next to Nancy." Frank gestures them together as he adjusts his camera. Nancy has on her all-white nursing uniform with her name tag and gold emblems on both sides of her uniform collar and hat. Standing side-by-side with each other's arms around their waists, they look like a pair.

Franks comments, "Jacqueline, they look so much alike. If Raina dyed her hair black, the two would almost look identical."

Nancy laughs. "Come on, big brother, take the picture. Some of us have school and work this morning."

Frank says, "Smile!"

The mother and daughter say together, "Smile!"

———

When Frank gets home from work, he enters the family study where Jacqueline is typing.

"Good evening, Jacqueline," he greets. "How was your day?"

He gives her a kiss on the cheek then sits down in the chair across from the desk.

"Pretty good, spunky, pretty good…"

Only the tapping of the typewriter keys fills the room until Frank sighs and leans forward, catching his wife's attention. "We received a letter from James Posey's attorney, Jeb Murphy, requesting a hearing to dismiss the suspension on his medical license."

Jacqueline looks up over the top of her readers and exclaims, "What!? Are you serious? This guy should never have the chance to get his medical license back. He shouldn't even be left alone with another person. He should be locked up and the key thrown away."

"I understand how you feel, and I agree. Attorney Proctor and his team are diligently putting together an argument as to why Posey should not get his medical license and why he should stay on probation." Frank leans back in his chair and proceeds talking. "Jacqueline, James Posey is coming to town in two weeks. Should we tell Nancy?"

The two look at each other for a moment and Jacqueline answers, "Nancy has finally gotten over the tragic incident. I really don't want to tell her that James Posey is coming to town. We don't know what that will do to her mentally."

Frank crosses his legs and replies, "It's a hard decision to make. As an attorney, I would want my client to know. I feel she needs to know as a brother, too, but things are going so well with her and Raina."

"How long will James Posey be in town?"

"One day. He's only here to get his suspension overturned."

As Jacqueline is about to speak, Nancy enters the room, sparkling, and says, "Good evening, Willoughbys! How were your days?"

Jacqueline replies, "Good, Nancy."

Frank says, "Pretty good, and yourself, spunky?"

"I'm doing great!" She sits down in the chair next to Frank, reaching up and taking the pins out of her hair to remove her nurse's cap. "It was a busy day. We had our morning communication meeting…and we're getting new beds for the second floor. Those things were so uncomfortable!" She claps her hands together. "It's great timing for Raina. There will be so many opportunities to move up at the hospital."

Jacqueline replies, "How's Raina doing these days? She has clinicals soon, right?"

"Yes, she starts next week. I will be giving a couple of seminars and a lecture for Raina's class. I'm assigning the students to their nursing instructor. I'm going to put Raina with Mrs. Scott, my old instructor. Mrs. Scott is the most knowledgeable nurse in the hospital." She stands up. "I'm going to go take a bath. Raina and I are going to the movies tonight."

"Nancy," Frank calls before she can leave the room. "I have something I need to tell you."

Before Frank can speak, Jacqueline quickly says, "Frank is about to tell you he wants to buy Raina a new car when she graduates from nursing school next year."

She catches Frank's eye and gives him a pointed, stern glance.

Frank pauses then replies, "Yeah, that's it."

"Oh, that sounds great! I was going to wait until after speaking with Raina, but since we are sharing good news, I have something to share with the both of you: I will be house hunting next week! Jacqueline, I want you to come with Raina and I house shopping."

Jacqueline gets up from the desk and gives Nancy a hug. "That's great, Nancy. I would love to go with you, but you don't have to move if you don't want. We love you living with us."

"I know, sis, but I'm ready to get back to being in my own house." She turns to them. "Thank you both for being there for me, twice. I'm so blessed to have the two of you in my life," says Nancy.

Frank stands up and gives her a hug. "Love you, little sister." He gives her a kiss on the cheek.

"Well, I'm headed to the shower," Nancy smiles as she leaves the room.

A moment later, Frank looks at Jacqueline and says, "I will tell her."

The next morning, Frank sits out on the back porch with Nancy and tells her that Dr. Posey is coming to town for a hearing to dismiss the suspension on his medical license.

Nancy looks at her brother and says, "Don't let that animal get his license back. Don't let him get it back." She gets up and goes into the house.

———

Raina begins her clinicals at Hillman Hospital. She and two other students are studying under Nurse Scott, a twenty-five-year veteran at the hospital. She has trained dozens of nurses in her career. Mrs. Scott always declined to become a floor supervisor, stating, "I'm not interested in supervising. My calling is to train others who want to be the best nurses they can be."

Raina comes to her for all her questions, including one about a patient in particular that's giving her worry. Mrs. Washington is really depressed about being in the hospital. Her husband is deceased, and her daughter just passed away; she has no family. Raina sits in her room and talks to her after classes each day.

"How do I lift her spirits?" asks Raina as she stands at the nursing station with Mrs. Scott, preparing medicine for her patients.

"Mrs. Washington is a wonderful woman. I've known her for years. She is a wealthy woman, especially now that she sold her house. She's outlived her family and friends, so she didn't want to linger on the memories. Form a friendship with her, show her love—genuine love—and pray with her."

Raina smiles and says, "Yes, ma'am".

———

That evening after the movies, Raina and Nancy go to the local hamburger joint to eat. As they enter, Raina sees a few of her friends there, and speaks to them briefly. When the two finally sit down in a booth, the waitress takes their orders and notes, "You two look so much alike!"

Nancy laughs. "Thank you so much for the compliment."

The waitress looks surprised and replies, "You're the mother! If you both had the same hair color, there would be no way to tell you two apart." She walks away, shaking her head in disbelief. Raina and Nancy laugh. They enjoy hearing they resemble each other.

"How do you like working at the hospital with Mrs. Scott?" asks Nancy.

The waitress comes back to the table with their Grapico sodas, then Raina replies, "I love the hands-on experience. The staff is interesting and fun, and Mrs. Scott even corrects the doctors! I saw her lecturing Dr. Smith about cleaning up his workstation; it was hilarious!"

"She is a wonderful woman. She is well-respected and probably knows more than some of the doctors at the hospital. Her bedside manner is superb, even with the most difficult patients. Always listen and do what is asked of you, and when it's time to take your certification exam, you'll pass it with flying colors."

"Yes, ma'am," says Raina as takes a sip of her soda through her straw.

"Enough about nursing. How's Concepción doing?"

As the waitress returns to the table with two plates, each with a hamburger and french fries, Raina answers, "She's doing great! She said the classes are tough, but she's maintaining an A average. Her new college friends are smart and helpful, and the professors are good. She'll be coming home next week, so I'm looking forward to seeing her."

Nancy replies, after taking a bite of her hamburger, "Please tell her she'd better see me before she goes back to school. That's great to hear she's enjoying the college life, though." She smiles and wipes the corners of her mouth with a napkin. She then resumes talking and says, "Raina, I have something exciting to say: I want us to start looking for our own house. What do you think?"

Raina eyes got big with excitement. "Yes, Momma! That will be fantastic!"

Nancy reaches over the table and holds Raina's hand and says, "I want us to live together in our own home. I want to be the mother that I always wanted to be to my daughter. I love you, Raina. I love being able to call you my daughter. Everything in

my life is so right! My career is flourishing, the hospital is growing, and I may be offered the position as head of nursing staff. I
have more friends in my life than ever, and my family loves me.
I'm ready to entertain again, having dinner parties for friends
and family. I want to decorate for the holidays, not with my
niece, but with my daughter." Nancy's eyes twinkle like the stars
and her entire face lights up, finally, as if reflecting the cool glow
of the moon against her dark backdrop of the past few years.

Raina looks into her mother's eyes and says, "It's good to see
you so happy, Momma!" They both laugh.

Chapter IX

DON'T CRY

MONDAY MORNING, APRIL 11TH, Jacqueline wakes up feeling something isn't right. She arrives at work, sits down at her desk, and begins working on her editorials.

Beat reporter Roger Hayes pokes his head into her office and says, "Jacqueline, I'm going down to the courthouse to cover the James Posey hearing."

She holds his gaze, expression grim. "Report everything you can. I'm counting on you." Right then, she realizes that's why she's feeling strange, but she shakes it off and focuses on her work. "Okay!" she says. "I want the story in the evening edition today."

"Will do, Mrs. Willoughby," says Roger as he swiftly walks through the newsroom. Jacqueline tries getting as much done as she can, but she has half her mind on Posey and one eye on the clock.

———

Proctor and Frank shake hands, and Frank says, "Great job, George! I really hope we have this one," he mutters, fingers quickly and incessantly tapping on the table.

"We have given Judge Roberts our expert letters, so there

should be absolutely no way he practices medicine again."

"I agree. Let's hope the judge sees it our way,"

"I'm sure he will," Frank reassures with a pat on Proctor's shoulder.

Four hours later, the courtroom is back in session. Judge Roberts hits his gavel twice. "I have reviewed all the documentation from both counsels and have reached my decision." He turns to the defendant. "Dr. James Posey, please stand. I'm overturning your sentence and order your medical license reinstated."

Proctor drops his head, chin almost touching his chest, and clenches his fists over the table. "Are you serious?!" he bursts out.

Judge Roberts hits the gavel and says, "You are out of order, counselor."

"Judge, this is a mistake!" Proctor hits his fist against the desk.

He hits the gavel three times and responds with a firm, loud voice, "You are out of order, counselor! One more outburst in my courtroom, and you will be held in contempt of court. I advise you to get a hold of yourself and leave my courtroom."

Frank grabs Proctor by the shoulders. "Calm down, George. Calm down. We'll request an appeal."

James Posey immediately hugs Attorney Murphy and says, "Thank you!" He shakes his hand then hugs his father.

"Told you everything would be alright," he says to his son. The three men leave the courtroom, victorious.

"I can't believe this is happening. This guy is clearly a criminal, and he gets off, first with a slap on the wrist, and now scot free," growls Proctor, muscles tense.

Frank replies, "I understand, but we can't give up. Tomorrow, let's get to the court house and appeal this decision and request a change of judge."

"Absolutely." The two lawyers gather their papers, put them in their briefcases, and slowly head out of the courtroom.

———

The three men do not answer any questions from the reporters at the courthouse. They quickly get into Murphy's car and speed off.

As Murphy takes the Posey family to the airport, Dr. Posey asks, "Mr. Murphy, could I inconvenience you to go by the Blach's department store? I would like to pick up a couple of shirts and ties. It's my favorite store; I love their necktie selection." Dr. Posey is riding in the passenger seat, so he looks over at the attorney with a slight smile. "I'm sure I won't be welcomed back to this city."

"I think we should go straight to the airport, but I guess one quick stop won't hurt," says Attorney Murphy.

"No problem. You guys have a few hours before your plane leaves, so do some shopping. Your dad and I can get a sandwich and finish up some business."

Murphy parks a half-block from the front entrance to Blach's, and the three gentlemen get out of the car. Mr. Posey and Murphy go inside a lunch cafe two doors down while Dr. Posey walks around the store for about thirty minutes, picking out a couple of shirts, ties, and hats. He makes his way to the counter and pays for his items then heads to the big glass double doors. As he exits the department store, five reporters with cameras and notepads meet him outside. The sidewalk fills with people walking in both directions in front of the store.

Roger Hayes steps up to Dr. Posey after following Murphy's car and says, "Dr. Posey, I'm Roger Hayes, a reporter from *The Birmingham Post-Herald Newspaper*. How do you feel about the decision made by Judge Roberts today?"

Dr. Posey, even though still startled by the reporters, answers, "I'm very pleased by the judge's decision."

"I would imagine, especially after only a slap-on-the-wrist sentence for assaulting a woman in her home. You only did six months in a mental hospital, now you've gotten the sentence dropped by Judge Roberts. Do you know the judge personally?"

Dr. Posey scowls. "Hey, don't be a wise guy! The judge made the decision, so get over it and get away from me."

Some of the people walking past stop to see what the commotion is about.

A reporter from the *Birmingham News* yells out, "Did your father's deep pockets and northern influences get Judge Roberts to overturn your soft sentence?"

"Who are you to judge!?" yells Dr. Posey.

Halfway down the block, Nancy and Karen are coming out of Butler's shoe store.

"Look, Nancy," Karen points to the commotion with a moderately concerned look. "I wonder what's going on there."

Nancy looks up from fiddling around in her shoe bag and says, "Probably some guys debating the war, who knows?"

As the two ladies get closer, the sidewalk traffic thickens and slows down due to people stopping to see what's going on. They can hear men arguing loudly back and forth. When Nancy and Karen approach the crowd, Karen says, "Let's go around."

So, Karen gets in front of Nancy as she pushes through the crowd. Karen shoves through to the edge of the sidewalk, Nancy close behind, looking in her shoe bag for something.

Suddenly, a yell rings out. "Get away from me!" The crowed opens up as Dr. Posey pushes people out of his way. He roars again. "Get out of my way!" Dr. Posey loses control of his emotions and what he is doing. He forces his way through the throng of people, knocking a couple bystanders down, including Karen. He turns to the next person, an unexpectant Nancy, and grabs her by the shoulders. She stares right into his fiery eyes, and Dr.

Posey freezes instantly. Nancy's eyes widen, and she drops her shoe bag. She screams. She jerks herself away from his grip and careens off the sidewalk, right out into traffic.

One man yells, "Stop, lady!" But there is the sound of screeching tires, and it is too late. A truck hits Nancy. Two men race out in the road to help her, and a couple more men run through the crowd, pushing back some of the gathering mob.

Karen runs into the street. "Nancy," she cries. "Someone, please call an ambulance!"

One of the men at the scene runs over to the phone booth.

Mr. Posey is facing the window inside the little diner and is distracted by the gathering people outside.

"What's going on out there?" He wonders as he stands to look out the window. Then he sees his son being pushed by some of the guys on the street.

He hurries out of the deli to get to his son. Murphy gathers up the paperwork off the table and rushes out behind Mr. Posey.

"What are you doing? Get your hands off my son!" Mr. Posey says to a couple of men harassing Dr. Posey.

Murphy screams as he pushes through the people, "James! Stop, get in the car! Don't say a word, James! Get in the car now!"

Dr. Posey, his father, and the attorney get into his car. Men are hitting the car with their hands as Murphy U-turns and drives away.

———

Raina is on the second floor giving medication to one of the patients when one of the nursing school students walks into the room and says, "Raina, you need to go down to the emergency room. I will finish giving Mrs. Weaver her medication."

She frowns, but hands her the medications. "Okay, but

what's going on, Debra?"

Debra looks at Raina with a disturbed look and repeats, "Go down to the emergency room." Raina just stands there for a moment, wondering what's going on, but she soon heads to the emergency room.

Raina feels there must be something terribly wrong when she sees her parents sitting outside of the ER, Frank with his head down and brows drawn together.

"Mother, Dad, what are you doing here? What's going on?" Raina asks as she walks up to them.

Frank stands up slowly, looks at Raina, and says, "Raina, Nancy is in that room. She was hit by a vehicle. Honey, it's not looking good."

Raina stands there in complete disbelief. "Dad, how did it happen? I need to see my momma." She turns to go into the surgery room, but Frank grabs Raina and pulls her into his arms. "I need to see my momma." Raina cries, tears running down her face.

"You can't go in there right now. Let the doctors work." Frank holds Raina as he fights back the tears.

Jacqueline puts her arms around both of them. "Let's pray."

Some of the staff members come down to the ER when they can, concerned about their boss, their coworker, their friend.

As time passes, they wait for someone to give them good news on Nancy's condition. After about an hour, Dr. Davis comes out of the emergency room. Dr. Davis slowly approaches the family, his expression grim.

Frank, Jacqueline, and Raina walk up to Dr. Davis, and Frank asks, "How's she doing, doc?"

With a look of deep worry on his face, he says, "I need the three of you to follow me." Dr. Davis ushers them through the double-doors to an office. "The three of you, please have a seat."

Dr. Davis squeezes the bridge of his nose and squints his eyes tightly shut. With a sigh, he opens them and puts his glasses back on. "Nancy has a lot of internal injuries, and she hit her head very hard on the ground. She has brain hemorrhaging. I'm sorry. There's nothing we can do."

Frank looks down at the floor for a second then at Raina, who has tears running down her face. Jacqueline's eyes also fill with tears.

Raina asks somberly, "How long does my mother have to live?"

Doctor Davis hesitantly answers, "A few hours, Raina."

"Is she conscious?"

"Yes," says Dr. Davis, "I had her taken up to a private room on the second floor. The three of you can go on up." The doctor walks to the door, but before exiting, he says, "I'm so sorry," as tears streak down his face.

The three leave and find Nancy's room. Frank opens the door, and Raina walks in first with Jacqueline behind her. Raina approaches the bed, looking at her mother lying there with her face swollen, scratched, and head wrapped in a bandage.

Raina holds Nancy's hand, wiping her eyes with her free hand. "Momma, Momma, can you hear me?" She then leans down and kisses Nancy on her red, swollen cheek.

Then, Nancy's eyes open halfway as she smiles weakly. "Baby, I'm so glad to see you."

Frank steps over to the opposite side of the bed Raina is standing on and says to his dying sister, "Nancy, we are here for you, sister. Everything is going to be all right."

Nancy smiles and croaks, "My dear brother, it's not going to be all right. I know I'm dying. I just thank God that He is letting me see my family, my daughter, before going to glory." Nancy turns her attention to Jacqueline. "Come over closer, sis."

Jacqueline walks up and stands beside Frank and holds

Nancy's other hand. "I love you, Jacqueline. You're like a sister to me."

Dora quietly enters the room and stands back, watching, careful not to disturb the family during this tough time.

"You both have always been there for me," Nancy speaks as her voice begins drying and cracking. "Frank, thank you for standing up for me when Mom and Dad put me out, giving me and my daughter a roof over our heads. You and Jacqueline protected my honor, you claimed my child as your own, and still made sure I was there to raise her. You both helped me finish high school and nursing school. You both helped me to become successful."

She then coughs and tries to talk, but her throat is so dry she can't speak. Raina quickly pours Nancy a glass of water. Nancy opens her lips as some of the water comes down her chin. Raina pulls the glass back, and pulls the sheet up to the bottom of her lip to wipe the water from her chin.

Tears fill Nancy's eyes, and her voice shakes. "Raina, my precious daughter. I know that I held a secret from you by not being forthright and telling you that I was your mother sooner. I'm so sorry. Will you forgive me?"

"Momma, you don't have to apologize. You've always been there for me."

"Please tell me you forgive me," Nancy says as she gives a slight moan of pain.

Raina sits in the chair next to the bed, smiles, and says, "Momma, I forgive you."

"Thank you, baby, I just needed to hear you say that." Her voice rasps even further as she slowly speaks, saying, "I want to tell you about your father, Francis. He was a wonderful person. He loved me; he gave me you."

"Momma, where is he now?" Raina asks as she gently

touches her mother's face with her fingertips.

"Raina, I don't know. He had to leave us." Nancy pauses and her gaze floats over Raina's shoulder, as if watching a movie on the wall. "I remember like it was yesterday, when he held you and kissed you on the forehead. He looked at me and said, 'You have given me another you. I love her, my daughter. I hope she grows up to look and be just like you, Nancy, my love.'" She slightly smiles. "He did say to me, 'I will always be near.'"

Tears stream down her face. "But they made him leave us. He had to leave us."

"Momma, stop crying," Raina begs as she holds both her mother's hands.

"Sing me a song, baby. Sing me 'Take My Hand, Precious Lord,'" Nancy weakly requests. Raina's lip wobbles, but she has to stay strong.

"Okay, Momma. I love you so much."

She sings:

Precious Lord, take my hand
Lead me on, let me stand
I am tired, I am weak, I am worn
Through the storm, through the night
Lead me on through the light
Take my hand, precious Lord
And lead me home.

Nancy opens her eyes, looks into Raina's, and says, "Thank you, baby. I love you." She closes her eyes and takes her last breath. Nancy has gone to be with the Lord.

Chapter X

I'M FREE

IT'S TEN O'CLOCK ON A CLEAR, warm Saturday morning. Family, friends, coworkers, and neighbors are at the Willoughby's home. They gather both inside and outside of the house, getting ready to go to the church for Nancy's funeral. Dean Morris, the funeral home director, and a couple members of his staff are walking around and giving their condolences.

Jacqueline is standing at the bedroom dresser mirror, putting on her earrings, and asks Frank while he ties his tie next to her, "Frank, have you noticed Raina being cheerful and happy since Nancy passed away? She has not once cried or even looked sad since Nancy's passing at the hospital. She's not grieving. What's going on with her? She's scaring me, Frank. Her mother has just passed, and she's carrying on as normal."

Frank took a minute to finish his tie before answering, "I've noticed the same behavior. She has picked out the casket, the burial plot, tombstone, and Nancy's outfit to be buried in. She's decided all the funeral arrangements with a smile."

Jacqueline sits down on the bed and says, "Frank, sit down and talk to me for a minute. We have time." Frank sits down next to her, then she asks, "Honey, how are *you* doing? I've seen you staring into space at times. What are you thinking about?"

Frank gives a reminiscent smile and replies, "I find myself thinking about my sister. Our ages being ten years apart, I remember when she came home from the hospital and holding her for the first time. Being there for her first steps, changing her smelly diapers." He then laughs. "She was always so beautiful and full of life, having a lot of friends, and so smart. The only time I ever saw her sad was when she found out she was pregnant. That's when Dad put her out of the house, and she went and stayed with Aunt Louise to give birth to Raina. Being her big brother, I felt obligated to take care of her and Raina. Jacqueline, thank you again for supporting my sister during that time. We gave her a fresh start, and she made the most of it. I keep thinking we should have told Raina that Nancy was her mother sooner." Frank drops his head.

Jacqueline lifts up Frank's chin and says, "Frank, you are a good man, a good father, and good brother. Nancy was very fortunate to have you. You were there for her every time it counted. You have nothing to regret. She loved you, Frank. I love you, and Raina does, too."

Frank stands up and grabs Jacqueline's hands, and she stands up. Frank hugs her and says, "I love you, Jacqueline." He gives her a kiss on the cheek, and Jacqueline gets her purse while Frank puts on his jacket. They head downstairs to join the others.

In the living room, Raina is reminiscing with family and friends about Nancy's life, telling stories about things she did to help people, how she positively affected lives, and was always uplifting and present. She is such a stylish young lady, getting it from her mother. She's wearing a wool black-and-gray plaid pencil skirt with a matching jacket, black silk blouse with a bow-tie collar, cashmere long gloves, black shoes, and a black cloche hat with a veil that flutters over her flawless makeup. Her long hair is pinned up in the back under her hat.

Concepción and her parents walk into the house, and Concepción walks over to Raina. She reaches out to hug her, but Raina only accepts the hug for a moment before gently pushing her friend away and saying, "I'm so glad to see you, sis," with a big, fun-filled look.

Concepción is puzzled about how her best friend could be so happy on the day they are burying her mother.

Raina interrupts her thoughts, "Where are your mom and dad? I want to talk to them before we leave for the church."

"They headed to the family room."

"Okay, sis." She leaves the living room to find them.

Jacqueline saw what happened, so she walks over to Concepción. "Hi, Concepción!" She gives her a big hug.

"You doing okay, Mrs. Willoughby?"

"I'm doing well. Concepción, has Raina talked to you about her mother's passing these last couple of days? Frank and I have noticed she hasn't grieved or even talked about Nancy's passing."

Concepción grasps Jacqueline's hand and leads her into a corner in the dining room. "Mrs. Willoughby, Raina has been exceptionally chipper. All she says is that her momma is in a better place now. When we went to the store to buy the outfit to bury Miss Nancy, she was shopping as if we were buying an outfit for her to wear out to a dinner party. She never had a sad moment. If it was my mother, I would be an emotional wreck."

One of the funeral director's assistants walks into the room. "Mrs. Willoughby," he calls, "it's time for the family to start gathering for prayer outside before getting into the limousine and going to the church."

"We are headed outside now, thank you," Jacqueline assures him then turns to Raina's friend. "Concepción, can you please ride with us in the family car? You are like a daughter to us, so sit with your sis during the service."

"Yes, I would be honored," she says as she gives Jacqueline a hug. "I love you, Mrs. Willoughby."

Everyone is outside. The funeral director stands on the front porch. "Everyone, I'm Dean Morris of Morris Funeral Home. Thank you all for coming to the homegoing service for Nancy Ann Willoughby. After prayer, my staff will escort the family to the limousines to be taken to the church. Everyone following in their cars, please follow behind with your lights on. Please bow your heads for prayer."

After a short prayer, the immediate family members proceed to get into the limousine cars. Other family members and friends get into their cars and follow the family to the church. The funeral procession begins.

The funeral procession approaches the red brick church at the end of the street. Both sides of the road are filled with cars, and the front and back of the church are overflowing. As the first of the three limousines stops near the stairs in front of the church, Frank, Jacqueline, Raina, Dora, and Concepción get out and walk upstairs. They enter the foyer, waiting to enter into the church.

The church is filled, standing room only, the white casket in front of the pulpit, open, Nancy laying there as if she were asleep. There are so many flowers surrounding the casket that the area looks like a flower shop. Nancy has on a black swing dress with a white wide collar and white sleeve cuffs with pearls around her neck. Her black hair cascades down her shoulders.

Raina walks down the center aisle of the church. Frank is to her left, Jacqueline on her right, with Concepción and Dora behind, followed by the rest of the large family. She stops in front of the casket, looking at her mother. Raina lightly touches her fingers to the sleeve of Nancy's dress.

The funeral director looks at Raina with pity. Concepción steps up next to Raina and says, "Sis, Miss Nancy is stunning! Let's sit down so the rest of the family can see her."

The five move over to sit in the front row to the left. Raina sits first, then Jacqueline, Frank, Dora, and Concepción. The rest of the family and friends view Nancy then sit down. Pastor Doyle presides over the funeral.

After the stirring homegoing sermon from Reverend Doyle, the choir stands up. The organ begins to play the song "Going Up Yonder." Concepción stands and moves in front of the piano. She sings.

> *If you want to know*
> *where I'm going,*
> *where I'm going, soon*
>
> *If anybody asks you*
> *where I'm going,*
> *where I'm going, soon*
>
> *I'm goin' up yonder*
> *I'm goin' up yonder*
> *I'm goin' up yonder*
> *to be with my Lord*

Concepción is singing with such somber passion that even the most stoic of listeners had to blink a few tears away. When they end the song, it takes a couple of minutes for the church to settle down. Concepción comes back over to her seat, and Raina gives her a big hug, saying, "Sis, that was beautiful! I love you!"

Reverend Doyle says, "Are we having a homegoing celebration or what?" He claps and turns around, looking at the other three ministers and the choir. He turns back around, facing the congregation, and says, "Amen. Sister Nancy is in heaven looking down on us, smiling. It's now time to move to the internment location."

The funeral director staff reopens the casket, rolls it down the middle aisle, and stops it just before the church foyer. "We want everyone in the back of the church to come around the side aisles around the front of the church and down the center aisle in a single line for the final viewing."

The family make their final goodbyes. Dora stops and says, "I'm gonna miss you, love." She takes a few seconds to gaze at Nancy while wiping her tears away with her white, red-flowered handkerchief. Concepción takes a last look at Nancy, saying, "Love you, Miss Nancy." Jacqueline and Frank stand there for a minute, looking at Nancy. Frank smiles at his little sister, and Jacqueline wipes her tears away.

Finally, Raina stands in front of the casket, looking at her mother with happiness. She touches her hair, running her fingers down her cheek, and lips, to the bottom of her chin. She puts her hand on Nancy's and says, "Momma, you have always made me feel special and loved. I love to hear when people say we look alike." Raina gives a silly laugh then says, "I promise I will make you proud of me. I love you, Momma." With both hands against her heart, she admires how lovely and peaceful her mother looks.

Mr. Morris says in a soft voice, "Miss Raina, we have to go." Raina stares for a couple more moments, then says, while still looking at her Momma for the last time, "She is so pretty. You would have loved the fragrance of her perfume." She then takes her black cloche hat off and puts it in the casket with Nancy, saying, "I almost forgot."

Jacqueline, Frank, and Concepción glance worriedly at each other before the family gets into the limousine to go over to the cemetery.

Everyone is around the casket with the immediate family sitting in the chairs up front at the grave side. Reverend Doyle, standing at the head of Nancy's casket, reads Ecclesiastes 3:1-8 then Genesis 2:7. He speaks of her spirit in the hands of the same loving God who tenderly cared for her in life. Reverend Doyle says, "Nancy Ann Willoughby has taken up the joys of eternal life. We therefore commit this body to the ground and this soul to the Lord. Earth to earth, ashes to ashes, and dust to dust, knowing full well that Jesus is the resurrection and the life. Please bow your heads in prayer. Almighty God, we gather beside this grave today to lay to rest the body of our friend and loved one, Nancy Ann Willoughby."

As Reverend Doyle prays, Raina's face begins to sadden, then tears run down her cheeks. Once Reverend Doyle finishes praying, the funeral director has the grave diggers begin lowering the casket into the ground. By this time, Raina is crying uncontrollably. She sobs, "Momma, Momma!" Then, all of a sudden, she yells out, "No! Momma, please don't go!"

The family tries consoling her, but she cries still. They can feel her deep pain. Raina never takes her eyes off the casket as it is being lowered into the ground. Jacqueline watches it descend, as well. She thinks of her amazing sister-in-law, her husband's only sister, and her daughter's mother being laid to rest.

As the family returns to the church for repast, Raina doesn't say a word. People speak to her, trying to get her spirits up, but she won't speak. She only nods or moves her shoulders. She won't eat, either. She just sits at the table and stares, nothing in her eyes.

Reverend Doyle comes over to the table, sits, and says, "Raina, is there anything I can do?"

Raina shakes her head.

"If you need anything, please let me know."

Concepción is sitting a couple of tables over with her parents when she notices Raina is still not speaking, so she goes over to the table and says, "Sis, come with me," as she takes Raina by the hand. They leave and go upstairs to the choir room.

"Sis, talk to me. I need to hear your voice. Say something, Raina," pleads Concepción.

Raina looks into Concepción's eyes and turns her head slowly side-to-side and begins to cry. Concepción places her arms around Raina as she lays her head on Concepción's shoulder. "I'm here for you, Raina. Sis is here for you."

Chapter XI

A CHANGE IS GONNA COME

THREE DAYS HAVE PASSED SINCE NANCY'S FUNERAL. On this chilly morning, Raina is sitting on the back porch, legs sideways on the seat, with an overcoat and skull cap wrapped loosely around her. Her head leans against the arm of the porch swing. Jacqueline walks outside and says, "Raina, I brought you a hot cup of cocoa." She reaches up to take the cup, sips out of it, and places it on the small stand on the side of the swing.

Jacqueline goes back into the house, and a couple of minutes later, she comes back out and places a quilt over Raina as she just stares into space. "Don't stay out here too long. Don't want you to get sick, okay?"

Raina never replies, just sinks down under the blanket, gaze blank.

Later, Frank and Jacqueline meet for lunch at Bogue's Restaurant.

"Frank, I'm really worried about Raina. She hasn't spoken a word since the funeral. She's always deep in thought, and I've tried talking to her several times, but to no avail. She won't speak. What are we going to do, Frank?" Jacqueline worries, biting her bottom lip.

As Frank is about to speak, the waitress brings out their food. Thanking her, she leaves the table.

Frank reassures, "I think we have to give her time to heal. She has been through a lot in the last year, and this is her way to deal with it." He takes a bite of his sandwich.

Jacqueline gives him an unimpressed look over the top of her glasses.

"I will talk with her tonight when I get home from work," says Frank.

She nods before her expression turns grim. "What is James Posey doing?"

"Right after the accident, he and his father got on a plane back to Boston. The police accident report states that Nancy was crossing the street and wasn't paying attention when she got hit by the truck," says Frank.

"Are you serious!? This guy gets away every time he breaks the law. Far as I'm concerned, he killed Nancy," Jacqueline replies in a sullen tone.

"We are trying to bring charges on James Posey. It takes time," says Frank.

"Someday, that guy will get his."

———

Raina sits on the couch in the living room, Nancy's framed picture from the coffee table in front of her. Dora walks into the room to dust and asks, "Raina, how are you doing?"

Raina responds by nodding her head. Dora sits down on the couch next to her and looks at the picture and says, "She was so beautiful, was so full of life, excitement, and her wit! Her style and taste in clothing was excellent. I really miss her, but she did leave us something. She left us her daughter." Dora looks at Raina and says, "We need you to be strong and beautiful like your mother. She would not be pleased to see you this way. We need to see her in you." Dora stands up and gives Raina a kiss on the forehead and says, "Love you," as she leaves the room.

Looking at her mother's picture, Raina smiles. Her mother wouldn't want her to be this way. Dora is right, she thinks. She would want her to be alive. Nancy is in her. She giggles at the thought.

Raina gets up off the couch and picks up the newspaper that is lying by the wooden staircase handrail. She sits down at the desk in the family library upstairs. Raina opens the newspaper, looking for the comic section, and stumbles across an article headline on the second page. "Dr. James Posey Medical License Reinstated."

Raina crumples the newspaper and throws it across the room. She leans her reddening cheeks into her palms, elbows on the desk, and her face tightens. She removes her face from her hands, her eyes blazing. Raina slams her fist on the desk and yells, tears gathering in her eyes, "You killed my momma!" She cries. After a few minutes, Raina retreats to her bedroom and shuts the door for the night.

Early the next morning, Raina comes downstairs with a small black box, grabs her sweater and car keys, and goes for a drive.

Raina drives a few miles out to the county where the Cahaba River runs through the deep valley. She gets out of the car with the black box. Finding a big rock to sit on down the hill from the road, she places the box on her lap and opens it. She picks up the picture of the red-headed man. "So, you're my father," she says.

Then, she picks up the gun, holding it flat in her hand. She opens the barrel, making sure it's not loaded. Raina takes two bullets out of the box and loads them into the small handgun. She walks over to the river and aims at a branch standing out of the water on the side of the bank. Raina fires the pistol twice.

"That was easy," she mumbles to herself, hitting her target. She gets two more bullets from her pocket to reload. After firing about ten rounds of bullets, she sits back on the rock.

Raina hears footsteps. Leaves crunch down the hill, and she turns around to see who it is. A young man with blond hair, very clean-cut, with a fishing rod and tackle box appears before her. As he comes closer, he says with a grin, "Hi! I heard you firing a few rounds, but I was surprised to see a pretty girl."

Beaming, Raina replies, "I was out shooting my mother's gun." He is the first person she has spoken to since the funeral.

"I was watching from my car and said to myself, 'She's a pretty good shot, and a hot pistol.'"

Raina smiles and says with a blush, "Thank you."

He smiles at her and says, "My name is Mark. What's yours?"

"Raina," she replies, giggling, and goes on to say, "It looks like you're going to do some fishing."

"Yes, I like to fish when I can, but due to my studies and part-time job, it's hard to get out here," answers Mark as he places his tackle box and fishing rod down.

"What school do you attend?"

"May I sit down?"

"Sure," answers Raina. Mark sits down next to Raina on the rock and answers, "Well, I'm a junior at Sanford University, and I major in pharmaceutical sciences. I want to be a pharmacist." He then looks Raina in the eyes and asks, "Are you in school?"

"Yes, my second year at Hillman School of Nursing. I'm following in my mother's footsteps." Raina trails off and focuses on the pictures in the black box.

Mark notices Raina's change in mood and asks, "What's wrong, Raina?"

Raina looks out at the river and says, "I lost my mother a week ago." She drops her head back down.

"I'm so sorry for your loss, Raina. I can't imagine how you feel. Remember, she's in a better place." He looks at her for a moment then down at the box of pictures on her lap and says, "Do you have a picture of her?"

She moves a couple of pictures aside and hands Mark one. He looks at it and at Raina and says, "Wow! It looks like you! Unbelievable; it's like you with black hair. She is gorgeous. Her daughter as well, of course." He hands the picture back with a wink, and Raina laughs.

He gets off the rock and extends his hand out, saying, "Hold this while I take a walk." Raina looks at Mark curiously, then she smiles, shaking her head, and reaches out to take his hand. Mark smiles and says, "I want to show you something." He leads her down the side of the rocky bank about forty yards until they get to a patch of white flowers.

Mark asks, "Have you ever seen these flowers before?"

"No, but they're so pretty," says Raina.

"They are the Cahaba Lily, only found here in Alabama, Georgia, and South Carolina. They grow to about three feet tall and lodge in between the rocks in the shoals. Would you like one?" asks Mark.

"Yes, but how? The flowers are about twenty feet out in the shallow water."

Mark takes his shoes off, rolls his wrangler jean pant legs up above his knees, and walks out toward the flowers. Once there, he picks three from between the rocks and wades back to the bank.

He reaches out and gives Raina the flowers. "For you, my dear."

Raina, flattered, says, "Thank you, handsome," as she takes the flowers and smells them.

"Raina, I think fishing will have to wait. I'm hungry." He laughs and bends down to put his shoes back on. "Would you like to join me? I know we just met, but I would be very interested in making a friend today. There's a little restaurant down the street that serves a killer-diller cheeseburger."

"Swell! I'll follow you." They gather their stuff and walk back up the hill, talking and laughing as they get into their cars and head over to the restaurant to eat.

Once Raina arrives home, she walks up the stairs to her room, but she stops in front of Nancy's old bedroom door. Raina absentmindedly says as she opens the door, "Hey, Momma, I just met—"

But no one is there.

She turns on the room light and reaches back to softly close the door. The room is undisturbed, no one even having entered since Nancy's passing. Raina sits down at the vanity and opens the drawer, taking out the hairbrush, and slowly brushes her hair. She beams, thinking about meeting Mark and how witty, fun, and full of life he is. As she looks into the mirror, she sees the picture of her and her mother side-by-side that's sitting on the nightstand behind her.

———

On Sunday morning, Jacqueline looks out the window, admiring the morning sunrise with her coffee in hand. As the sun slowly ascends, a familiar voice breaks her out of her reverie. "Good morning."

Jacqueline turns around, and her coffee cup shatters on the floor. "Oh my goodness. Nancy," gasps Jacqueline as if she were looking at a ghost.

"No, Mother, it's me, Raina." She laughs.

Dora hears the crash and walks into the kitchen, catching sight of Raina. "Lord," she says, placing her hand on her heart.

Raina offers, "Let me get that broken cup and coffee cleaned up." She collects the broom and dustpan from the closet.

Jacqueline addresses Dora and says, "Are you seeing what I'm seeing? Raina has gone to the hair salon and had her hair dyed, and she is dressed exactly the way Nancy would dress. Raina looks just like Nancy when she was a girl."

"Mrs. Willoughby, I thought I saw a ghost," says Dora, her face drawn.

"Did you hear her voice? She sounds like Nancy, Dora."

Dora sits down with Jacqueline and Raina for breakfast. Once they finish, Raina stays in the kitchen to wash the dishes while Dora puts them away. Frank doesn't come downstairs for breakfast, staying upstairs to finish up some work for a deposition on Monday morning.

Jacqueline and Raina load up in the car, waiting for Frank so they can head to church. Moments later, he rushes into the driver's seat of the car and says, "Sorry, everyone! Let's go praise the Lord."

Frank is just about to put it in gear when he looks up into the rear-view mirror and notices Raina, a purple cloche hat sitting atop her black hair with a beautiful smile on her face. Frank just stares in astonishment.

"Frank…Frank…" calls Jacqueline.

"Father, we're going to be late for church," Raina prods as she leans forward and kisses Frank on the cheek.

He blinks. "Okay, right, let's go," replies Frank as he looks over at Jacqueline in astonishment. She sends him a worried glance before he leaves for church.

The three arrive, and Raina, out of the car first, says, "I will meet you two in there. I want to speak with Reverend Doyle before service starts."

As Raina enters the church, passing people outside stop to whisper comments like, "She looks just like Nancy."

As soon as she's gone, Frank turns to his wife and says, "What is going on? Raina dyed her hair, and her voice...she sounds like Nancy. What has happened?"

"I'm seeing the same things you are, Frank. I can't explain it."

He sighs. "Let's get into church before we're late."

Chapter XII

EVERY TONGUE SHALL CONFESS

RAINA RETURNS TO SCHOOL TO FINISH HER CLINICALS at the hospital. A couple of weeks later, she is assigned to the nursing home to train. As she works around the home, she gets to know all the patients there. They all love her bedside manner, passion, and care.

Unfortunately, a few of the residents begin to complain about their items missing. Miss Allen and Miss Cooper tell Raina their jewelry is missing, and Mr. Walter, whose wife passed a couple of months ago, tells Raina, "All I had left of my wife was the bracelet she wore for over sixty years. I gave it to her on our first wedding anniversary. I kept it in my top drawer. I'd only taken it out once since her recent passing. I missed her, and now it's gone." He weeps.

Raina places a comforting hand on the old man's shoulders. "You will get her bracelet back, Mr. Walter. We will find it." She smiles at him then gives him a big hug.

Lyle, one of the orderlies, is in the laundry room folding towels when Raina walks in to get some towels for the nurse's station.

"Raina, I've been wanting to ask you something."

"What's up, Lyle?"

"You are very lovely, and I see you like nice things," Lyle

says as he stops folding towels. He walks over and stands behind Raina.

"What are you getting at, Lyle?" She stands there, waiting for his reply.

Lyle gets close to Raina, putting his lips close to her ear, and whispers, "We're all friends, and I spoke with the others—Max, Jane, and Emily—and we want to let you in on something. We feel we can trust you; we've all known each other since we were kids. We're taking some of these old folk's jewelry and valuables. I've got a man in Georgia that gives us good prices on the stuff." Lyle puts one hand on Raina's shoulder and says, "I was wondering if you wanted in. You're close to a lot of the patients and could help us get the really valuable stuff." He rubs her shoulder slowly.

She looks at Lyle's hand on her shoulder, then replies, "It doesn't bother you, taking the old-timers' valuables?"

"Not at all. What are they going to do with it? Let someone young enjoy it," he answers with a smirk on his face. Lyle then steps around in front of Raina and says, "You're a hot babe, and I want you to be my girl."

Raina gives a hesitant half-smile and walks out of the laundry room. Raina catches the elevator headed to the hospital's HR department to report what Lyle had told her, but when she arrives, the department door is closed. She plops down in the chair in the waiting area outside the office door. She ponders what to do. Those scammers have broken a lot of these senior citizens' hearts. If she tells, they'll only be fired and may even go to jail, but those people won't ever get their precious items back.

She continues to think about how bad people are getting away with doing bad things to good people. Her eyes burn with the swelling tears, and she begins to cry. Raina thinks they're disgusting, every one of them. These sweet, old patients are innocent, and her fellow coworkers, people she and the patients should be able to trust, are stealing something from each of them.

She curls up, her forehead touching her thighs, and threads her fingers through her hair, shielding her from the harsh light of the empty hallway.

She cries uncontrollably for a minute then stops, sits up straight, and wipes the tears from her eyes to reveal a face drained empty of all that was in her. The expression flickers to one that can kill, but quickly straightens.

"Something has to be done to these yucks! I'm going to have to give it to them myself. I'm going to clip them," she vows.

She resolutely stomps back to the laundry room, where Lyle is sleeping, head on the table. Raina walks up and softly places her hand on the back of Lyle's neck. "Lyle, I was thinking… and you're right. I want to be a part of the scheme," says Raina.

"Good choice. I knew you couldn't resist a great opportunity and being around me, of course," Lyle says arrogantly. He continues, "We'll be meeting at my uncle's house on Saturday. You can see some of the stuff we have. Until then, find out where they keep anything of value and where the old-timers are hiding their stuff."

She agrees and turns to go back her patients, but Lyle pats Raina on the butt and says, "You're a hot dish."

She stiffens, but turns with a smile and says, "Not as hot as I'm going to be for all of you Saturday." She winks at Lyle. As soon as she's out the door, her expression turns from pleasant to disgust.

On Saturday evening, Raina arrives at Lyle's Uncle Vinny's secluded riverside home in Locust Fork wearing her cloche hat. She gets out of the car and walks up to the front door with her hands in her jacket pockets. She closes her eyes and lowers her head for a moment, then opens her eyes, looks up at the door, and smiles as her eyes shine. She then says to herself, "Showtime."

Raina knocks on the door, and moments later, Lyle opens the door, a smirk already plastered on his face.

"Raina, what a pleasant surprise. And here I was just thinking how nice it'd be to spend a little while with you," he says, wearing a lustful grin. Raina stands, smiling. Lyle steps out onto the porch and shuts the door behind him. "We've got a lot of the keepsakes, jewelry, and money from those old folks at the nursing home here in the house," he says as he gets up close to Raina.

"You have a girlfriend," Raina says. "Emily."

"Emily doesn't compare to you; I'd drop her in a minute if you gave me a chance," Lyle says.

"What about Alexander? He's my boyfriend," replies Raina.

"What about him? I don't care about him. I want you." Lyle steps forward and puts his hands on her waist. Raina stands there, her hands still in her jacket pockets. "I've wanted you for a while." Lyle sighs.

Raina looks into his eyes and asks, "Do you think I'm pretty?"

"Pretty?" Lyle grins. "You're gorgeous."

Raina asks, "Do you like the fragrance of my perfume?" She takes a step closer to him.

Lyle leans forward, placing his face close to Raina's neck and says, "Yes," the tip of his nose now touching Raina's neck as she just stands there, still. Lyle stands straight and looks into Raina's alluring eyes. Raina's enchanting smile suddenly changes to fury as her eyebrows pull together, eyes glare, lips tightly close and become thinner, and her face reddens. In an instant, Raina pulls a knife from under her jacket and jams it into Lyle's racing heart.

Lyle stands there for a few seconds, looks down at the knife, back into Raina's eyes, then drops to his knees. Raina puts her left hand on the back of his neck and uses the right to pull the knife out of his chest. She then jams it back in, holding him against her, and pulls the knife out before taking a step back. She takes the bloody knife, slides it sideways across the side of his shoulder to wipe the blood off then wipes the opposite side of the blade off on the other shoulder. She places the blade back in its leather case under her jacket and gazes down at him. He is holding his hands over the stab wounds in shock, but she merely steps to the side and walks past. Before she goes too far, she reaches back and pushes his head forward; Lyle's body collapses, his face hitting the porch with a *thunk*.

Raina then goes in through the front door, closing it shut and locking it. She quickly strips off her jacket and long skirt to reveal a clean blouse and another, shorter skirt free of blood.

Raina notices a hat rack next to the door, so she takes her red cloche hat off and hangs it there. As Raina walks into the living room, she hears a male voice yell from upstairs, "Hey! Did anyone hear that noise? Sounds like it was from outside." She recognizes it as Max's.

A girl's voice answers, "Yeah! I heard it."

Raina follows the girl's voice to the open layout family room, where two girls sit at the table going through the stolen jewelry.

"Sorry!" Raina sheepishly raises her hand. "That was me."

One of the girls, Jane, looks up. "Raina, you made it; good to see you here," she says excitedly, bright-eyed and with a huge smile.

"Hi, Raina, I knew you would join us," says the girl sitting opposite, Emily. She's holding a watch that Raina knows belongs to one of the doctors at the nursing home that came up missing a week ago.

"Where is Max?" asks Raina as she approaches the table, picking up some of the items on the table to examine them more closely.

Emily replies, "He is upstairs, getting the money out of Uncle Vinny's safe. Vinny and his wife will be back tomorrow, so we are moving all the stuff out. We are also heading to Georgia to sell everything."

Raina walks to the staircase, turning toward the table where the girls are sitting, and leans against the handrail. "Does it bother you that stealing elderly and sick patients' things is wrong?"

Jane replies, "No! This money is too easy. Working at the nursing home doesn't pay enough."

Emily follows, "Raina, look, this locket is from Miss Davidson. She is loaded and can afford to buy another one."

Raina pauses for a moment, and replies, "That locket has more sentimental value than you know."

"Sounds like you have a problem with what we're doing. Why are you here, Raina?" Emily cuts in, glaring at her.

"Yeah, Raina, you got a problem with this?" asks Jane as she stands up at the table.

A tall, slim guy comes down the stairs and asks, "Where's Lyle?"

"He's out on the front porch," Raina replies.

Max stands at the bottom of the stairs next to Raina and asks, "What's the problem down here?"

Emily answers, "Raina's standing there and saying we're wrong for what we're doing!"

"Raina, why the heck are you here if you don't want to be a part of our business?" Max asks crossly, folding his arms.

Raina looks straight at Max and says, "I'm here to get Miss Davidson's locket, and since I'm here, I will also take the others' stuff."

"You aren't going to take anything from here," says Jane as she steps from around the table.

Emily responds angrily, "You are pretty stupid to come in

here and tell us what you're going to do. Take the merchandise from us? That's not going to happen, pretty girl."

"So, you don't believe me? Watch this, girls." Raina smiles. In a blink of an eye, Raina pulls a gun out of her jacket pocket, puts it against Max's temple and shoots. Max's head jerks to the side, and he falls against the staircase banner and down to the floor. Jane and Emily start screaming frantically upon seeing Max's death.

"Shut up and get down on your knees, now!" Raina orders.

Jane and Emily cry and fall to their knees.

"I said shut up, girls!" Raina turns the gun in their direction. They go quiet fast.

Raina pulls two pairs of handcuffs out of her skirt pocket and toss them at their feet. "Crawl over and cuff yourselves to the furnace pipes in the corner, now!"

Raina uses her free hand to pick through the items on the table. "Now, what did you say about me not taking Miss Davidson's locket and the other items back to the nursing home?" Raina runs her hand over each item. "So, let me see. We have rings, necklaces, watches, bracelets, and money. You four are despicable scum! How could you do this to the elderly?" Raina picks up a handful of jewelry and slams it back down.

Emily stares at the lifeless Max laying on the floor, his eyes halfway open and blood running from the gunshot wound to his head, and asks while crying, "Where is Lyle?"

Raina looks up from the table of stolen goods and answers, "Like I told you, he's *out* on the front porch."

Jane cries, "Help!" She drops her head down, sobbing.

Raina walks over, stands behind her, and hollers, "You scream one more time, just one more time, Jane…"

But Emily's sobbing only grows louder as she asks, "Why… why…why did you kill my Lyle?"

Raina says, "Let me tell you, Emily: that guy really didn't care about you; he only cared about what you could do for him and what he could get out of and from you."

Jane keeps staring at Max, crying and quivering. She screams again, "Help!"

Raina walks behind Jane and bends forward, putting her face close to Jane's ear and the pistol against the back of her head. She whispers, "I told you not to scream again, and you did. Bye-bye, Jane."

Raina keeps the gun drawn and reaches under the side of her blouse, pulls the knife from its leather case, places the blade against Jane's neck, and slashes her throat. Jane falls forward, choking on her own blood.

Emily watches in shock even as Raina asks, "Do you have anything you want to say, Emily?" There's a devilish smirk on her lips.

Raina looks back at Jane and watches as blood runs out onto the floor. Raina takes the edge of the table cloth, cleans the knife off, and slides the knife back in its case on her hip.

Raina says, "I read that slitting someone's throat accomplishes three things: severing the trachea generally below the larynx, which prevents screaming. Accomplished. Second, it severs the carotid artery, preventing new oxygenated blood from reaching the brain. On track. Lastly, it severs the jugular vein, allowing blood to flow easily from the brain; that's happening now. She's unconscious, so death will follow shortly."

"You are crazy! Help her, Raina!" Emily begs.

"Help? Help her?" Raina points to the dying woman between them. "Help, like she helped all those old folks at the nursing home? No! Instead, she teased them, insulted them, and stole from them. She's getting what she deserves." Raina turns back to Jane and says, "It's been about a minute, so, due to the blood loss and lack of oxygen, Jane is now dead."

"Now, Emily," Raina begins with the bearing of a teacher instructing a dull pupil. "Tell me why the four of you decided to mistreat and steal money from the elderly." Emily just stares at Jane, not looking at Raina.

"I was only doing what Lyle told me to do," Emily responds in a trembling voice.

Raina shoves her face close to Emily's face and yells, "So, if he told you to jump off a cliff, you would have done it? I don't want to hear your lies!" Raina storms across the room to compose herself, counting backwards and taking deep, slow breaths. After a minute, she walks back over to Emily and says, "I'll tell you what...if you can answer this riddle in one minute, I will leave. Let's say I will give you a pardon, but if you don't answer it correctly..."

Emily somberly asks, "What's the riddle?"

"What can you serve, but never eat? Now, you have one minute to answer the riddle." Raina walks over to the small kitchenette in the corner of the room and opens the cabinets above the countertop, looking for a glass. Opening up the refrigerator, she exhales. "Ahh, a Coke."

Raina calls to Emily, "Where is the bottle opener? Never mind, its hanging here on the cabinet knob." She takes the bottle opener, opens the bottle of Coke, throws the cap in the trash can next to the refrigerator, and takes a sip.

"H—How can you be drinking a *Coke*," Emily cries, tears running down her face, "when you've just *killed everyone*?!"

"You have thirty seconds."

"Please, help me! Help! Help!" screams Emily.

"You better figure out the answer to the riddle, girl. While you've been making a bunch of noise, you now only have fifteen seconds left to go," reminded Raina.

"No, Raina, please don't kill me. Please don't kill me," Emily begs for her life.

"What's the answer to the riddle, Emily? What's the answer?" Raina asks in a casual voice.

"I—I don't know." Emily whimpers, body trembling. She's muttering the riddle under her breath, chest heaving.

"Ten."

"Please, Raina, don't kill me."

"Nine. Eight."

"I don't know! I can't think!

"Seven. Six…" Raina counts down, looking at her watch.

Emily pleads, "Just take everything and leave. I promise I won't tell anyone, I promise!"

"Two."

"Help!" Emily breaks down, dropping her head and whimpering.

"One." Raina sips some soda, places the bottle on the counter, and continues, "I'm very offended you don't know the answer to that riddle." She walks over and bends down on one knee with the gun pointed at Emily.

"Again, what can you serve but never eat?" She pauses. "A tennis ball, you silly goose! Everyone that plays tennis knows that riddle, except you, I see," says Raina. "Well, Emily, I have to get all this stuff packed up and get it back to its rightful owners. It was nice speaking with you."

Raina passes behind Emily, then stops, places the gun behind Emily's head, and pulls the trigger. Emily's head falls forward, hitting the radiator heat pipes, and she falls sideways onto the floor.

"Wow! Look at all the blood," Raina says to herself, shaking her head and walking out the room.

Raina rummages through the house, gathering all the money

and the valuables that were taken from the elderly at the nursing home. She puts everything in the box except for the money.

"I'm going to keep the cheese; may need it for a future trip."

Raina walks to the front door, placing the box on the chair next to the door. She puts her cloche hat back on, picks up the box, and goes out the door, closing it behind her and stepping over Lyle's lifeless body laying out on the porch.

Raina gets home about an hour later, leaving the box of items in the trunk of her car, goes upstairs, and sits down at Nancy's vanity desk. She tosses her hat on the bed.

Raina is euphoric as she looks at her momma's picture, grinning at the amazing feelings overtaking her.

She smiles then hysterically laughs as she takes off her clothes and places them in a bag to burn later. Raina sits down, her eyes locked on the picture. She opens the vanity drawer, taking out Nancy's old hair brush, and brushes her hair, saying, "My heart was hardened, and all my tears went away. Vengeance was sweet."

Monday morning, Raina arrives at the nursing home to finish up her last week of clinicals. As she is feeding one of the patients, Helen, another nurse, pokes her head in and says in a somber voice, "Raina, did you hear about Emily, Lyle, Jane, and Max?"

"No," replies Raina.

Helen walks next to Raina and whispers, "They were found killed in Lyle's uncle's river house Sunday afternoon."

"I'm sorry to hear this."

As she resumes feeding her patient, Helen frowns, surprised that Raina seems unconcerned about the four deaths.

The following day, Nurse Perry places a box on the nurses' desk. "There was a box outside the back entrance of the nursing home."

The box reads, "Give these precious contents back to their rightful owners." Nurse Perry opens up the box and takes out necklaces, watches, rings, and different keepsakes. Raina and a couple of the student nurses stand around the counter, watching Nurse Perry take the items out of the box.

"I wonder who left this box," says one of the training nurses.

Raina says, "That locket looks like Miss Davidson's missing locket."

Student nurse Judy picks up one of the watches and says, "I think this is Dr. Adam's missing watch."

Nurse Perry, looking astonished at all the items, adds, "I think this is all the stuff that was missing from our patients. Who returned them?" She looks curiously at the box.

Raina interrupts, "If it's the stuff that our patients are missing, can we go around and give it back to them?"

Nurse Perry says enthusiastically, "Absolutely! Raina and Judy, the two of you go around and ask each person if they're missing anything, and if so, have them describe it so we can return it. I'm sure it will make them happy. These are their valuable memories."

Chapter XIII

RIGHT ON TIME

HERE'S A KNOCK AT THE DOOR, so Dora rushes over from the kitchen to answer. "Oh my goodness," she gasps.

"Hello, Dora." Alexander reaches out and gives her a hug.

"I'm so glad to see you! You are looking well," says Dora.

Alexander is back from the war due to a gunshot wound to the leg he suffered in combat. Raina comes out from the study to the stairs and looks down to see Alexander in his marine uniform. She immediately leaps down the stairs to Alexander and hugs him tightly. She gives him a big kiss on the lips.

"I'm glad you're home. I've missed you!" says Raina excitedly.

Frank and Jacqueline enter into the living room, and Jacqueline walks up to give him a hug. "My goodness, Alexander! I'm so glad you're back home."

Frank steps up and shakes Alexander's hand, giving him a hug, as well, and says, "Welcome home, young man. Good to see you back well."

Everyone sits down in the living room, and Alexander tells a few stories about what happened over in Europe and East Asia. After about an hour, Frank and Jacqueline give Alexander one more hug then both retire upstairs.

Raina, sitting next to Alexander, reaches an arm around

him and kisses him softly on the lips.

"I missed you so much, Alex," she says, looking into his eyes.

"I missed you so much. I thought about you every day there." He runs a hand through her hair. Taking a strand, he asks, "Raina, why did you dye your hair? You look just like Nancy." He releases the hair and kisses her forehead. "I'm so sorry she passed."

"Thank you, Alex. It's been hard, but...I'll be okay," says Raina as she sidles closer to Alexander. "Baby, I dyed my hair black because it was time for a change. It's motivation for me to do what's necessary, to right the wrongdoings."

"Raina...are you okay? You...you seem different. Angrier," says Alexander with an inquisitive look on his face.

"Well, like I said, sweetheart, I'm a changed woman." She grips his shoulders. "Let's talk."

———

One day, while the family is lounging in the family room to read, Raina finds a newspaper article on page three. "Doctor Posey Wins Boston's Doctor of the Year Award."

Her grip tightens on the paper. She reads about the ceremony, about the standing ovation, and about his sickening comment ("All those who falsely accused me, I forgive you.").

Raina's face is overwhelmed with anger as she looks at the photo of Dr. Posey standing at the podium, the mayor and his father on either side of him. As Raina looks at the picture, she thinks about that murderer claiming to be self-righteous as he accepts his award.

She thinks to herself, "Dr. Posey, all mushrooms are edible, but the right one will kill you."

She smirks, closing the newspaper and sitting back in the

chair in thought.

———

Jacqueline and Frank are gone to a theater show while Raina is home for the evening. Mark arrives at the house and is greeted by Dora at the door. "Good evening, young man. May I help you?"

"Going evening. I'm here to see Raina."

Dora replies, "Is your name Mark?"

"Yes, ma'am," he says.

"Come on in, Mark, and have a seat on the couch. Raina is expecting you. I'm going to let her know you're here. Would you like a Coke, sweet tea, or some lemonade?" she offers.

"No, ma'am, but thank you," Mark replies.

Dora nods her head and leaves. Mark sits on the couch and surveys the big, well-furnished room with seventeenth-century paintings over the fireplace. The padding of feet catches his attention, and he looks to the top of the staircase where Raina stands. Her black hair perfect and curved body in jeans and a pink flowered blouse. This is Mark's first time seeing her with makeup, which is flawless. He stands up from the couch in awe of Raina's beauty.

"Say something, Mark," says Raina as she walks down the staircase, giggling.

He takes her hand and kisses the back with a playful grin on his face. "I shouldn't be surprised. You look even lovelier this time."

He walks over to the mantle and picks up the picture of Nancy. Raina walks closely up to Mark, and he catches a whiff of her perfume. "Wow! You smell wonderful."

"Thank you, Mark," replies Raina, smiling, then continues wistfully, "She was a wonderful mother and a woman who dedicated her life to helping people."

"Would you mind telling me about her? I would love to know more."

"Sure, let's sit down on the couch, and I'll tell you all about her," Raina says, and Mark can't help but stare at her mesmerizing beauty. She reaches over and holds Mark's hand, as he is taken with her beauty and fragrance.

Raina tells Mark all about her mother, as well as the family and herself. Mark tells Raina all about his family, friends, and his high school years. They find they know some of each other's friends.

"Mark, since it's too late to beat you in a match of tennis, do you know how to play chess?"

Mark lifts one eyebrow and replies, "Do I! I was co-captain of my high school chess team."

"I was also a member of my school's chess club team, so I'm pretty good myself," she admits, then turns to him with a playful simper. "Could I challenge you to a game of chess, sir?"

"Yes, let's play!"

"Let's go up to the family room and match wits," Raina says. She stands and extends her hand. "Hold this while I walk upstairs."

Mark smiles, getting a taste of his own witty medicine, as he grabs her hand and follows her up.

The two sit across from each other and study the chessboard. Mark makes a move on the board, and Raina smirks. Raina makes a move, and Mark smirks. This rhythm continues, and the pieces dwindle down for each.

"Check," Mark says, smugly crossing his arms.

"This looks bad," she says as she focuses on the chess board. After a moment, Raina says, "Mark, let's make a deal. If you win, I will sing you a song, but if I win, you'll do a favor for me."

"Okay, but I don't think you'll get a favor from me because I have this game won already. But if you insist, yes, let's make the deal." He holds out his pinky finger. Raina curls her finger around his, and they shake.

As soon as they let go, Raina says, "You never make an open-ended deal with an attractive woman. Checkmate!"

Mark blinks at her then turns to the board, scratching his head. "Huh." He laughs. "Well, what's the favor?"

"Let's go into my bedroom first," suggests Raina.

"What about Miss Dora?" asks Mark.

"She's gone home for the night, so it's just you and me." She teasingly pokes his arm. "Are you afraid to be alone with me, Mark?" Her eyes are dramatically wide, and when he doesn't immediately respond, she bursts out laughing. "Come on!"

Raina opens the door to her bedroom and says, "Brawns and blond before beauty and brains," as she chuckles.

Mark grins and walks into her room, shaking his head. "I'm rubbing off on you, Raina."

He walks in, looking around the room. Her room is neat, painted a crisp white. The red and green flowers of her queen-sized bed match the window drapes, and her desk is orderly, as if it were a corporate office desk. Her vanity of makeups and perfumes, the latter lightly scenting the room with flower bouquets, is arranged meticulously. The mantel is covered with all her trophies, placards, and certificates from over the years, as well as her tennis racket and letterman sweater.

"This is amazing!" Mark comments, focusing on the mantel. "You are also athletic and smart." He gazes around the room further, but when he turns around, Raina stands face-to-face with Mark. She winds her arms around his neck and presses her lips to his.

"And pretty," he adds after the kiss finishes. The two begin kissing again until Raina moves her hands from around Marks neck, lightly pushing against his chest.

"This is my favor: I want you to get me a very powerful injectable sedative from the hospital."

"Why?" Mark replies with a curious look.

"I can't say why, but you promised. You lost the bet, and you promised you would make good on it," Raina says as she slowly runs her fingers through his hair then kisses him on the lips.

"I can get in a lot of trouble over this. I could go to jail."

She frowns in disappointment. "I guess we better go downstairs," says Raina.

"Let me think about it," replies Mark as he stands there for a moment, wondering why she is asking for the sedative. Raina turns and walks out of the bedroom with Mark closely behind her. The two resume their conversation downstairs on the couch.

Ten o'clock comes. "It's that time, Mark. I really enjoyed you this evening," says Raina as they walk to the front door hand-in-hand.

"Thank you so much for a heck of a time. I think you are a swell girl," says Mark.

"Thanks," she smiles. "You're not so bad yourself," says Raina. "Don't forget you lost a bet, though. I need to know if you're going to get the sedative for me."

"I'm a man of my word, so I will make good on the bet."

"I know you will." She smiles. "Good night." She kisses Mark softly on his lips.

"Good night, Raina." Mark beams as he walks away, and Raina slowly shuts the door behind him.

She turns, placing her back against the door, pausing in thought for a moment then saying, "I feel Mark is falling in love with me. I hope he knows what he's getting into." She walks away from the door, chortling. "He's rubbing off on me."

———

"Hello, sis!" greets Concepción as she opens her dorm for her friend. The two girls hug, and Concepción notes, "You dyed your hair black." She stands back, scrutinizing Raina. "Scary. You look identical to Aunt Nancy."

"Everyone tells me that. I just wanted a change," replies Raina then leans toward the door. "Let's go, girl. I'm hungry after this hour and a half drive."

"Let's go!" Concepción agrees, and they walk over to the college's local restaurant. They sit in a corner booth.

"So, what's been up with you?" asks Concepción.

"I'll be graduating school here in the coming months and hopefully will start working at the hospital full time," says Raina.

Concepción nods. "Just one year left, and I graduate. I'm ready to get back home. I miss everyone."

"I miss you, too!" says Raina. Her face then shifts, serious, and she leans forward. "Sis, I need to talk to you. I need some advice."

"I'm all ears," says Concepción.

As Raina places her elbows on the table, she says, "I told you in my last letter that I met a guy named Mark. He's amazing, sis! He's polite, funny, witty, and smart."

"So, what about Alexander? You and he have been together for years. Sounds like you are ready for a change," says Concepción.

Raina pauses for a moment. "I have always cared about Alex. He's a gentleman, handsome, and smart. Now that he's back from the war, though, he's looking to marry, and I'm not. Mark, on the other hand, is a wonderful guy, and he has expressed he wants us to be a couple." Now, what comes out of Raina's mouth really surprises Concepción. "Sis, I've been through a lot the last couple of years. I'm a different woman. I've learned that I have to take things into my own hands to get the results I want. Selfish, arrogant, and downright evil people took my mother from me. I had faith in the judicial system, but I found out that money and power rule. Those responsible will get theirs, and they will pay." Her eyes fill with fire, and her face darkens.

"Sis, are you okay?" asks Concepción hesitantly.

Raina puts her face in her hands and composes herself. She then looks right at Concepción with a smirk on her face, her whole demeanor changing. "Yes." She nods. "What are you having to eat?"

As she picks up the menu, Concepción looks at Raina with a look of concern, but she then glances down at her menu and says, "I'm getting the cheeseburger plate."

"Oh! Cheeseburger? That sounds pretty good! I'm thinking of getting a club or something."

The girls eat lunch and talk for a couple of hours, updating each other on school, family, and friends.

Concepción asks, "So, what are you going to do about the guys? Which one are you going to date?"

She leans forward, folding her hands in front of her, and says with conviction, "They will have to compete to get the prize, and the game has already started. Who will do whatever it takes to have me? Whatever it takes."

Concepción listens anxiously to this person before her because it's not the Raina she knows.

———

Raina and Alexander take a walk through the forest at the back of his parents' house to the stream that holds small fish, craw-fish, frogs, and the occasional turtle. The two wander about fifty yards along the creek until they find a secluded, hidden-away area in the curve of the creek that goes into the brush and thick-ness of the forest. This is where Alexander sits for his quiet time. He had brought Raina here a couple of times to sit on the old oak tree that fell years ago due to a severe storm. Now, it rests perfectly beside the mellow creek. They sit down on the make-shift bench.

As the two watch the water run peacefully downstream, Raina turns to Alexander and asks him, "Would you do any-thing for me, Alex?"

"Yes, Raina. Why do you ask?" he answers.

Raina looks at his lips then up into his eyes. "I have a favor to ask of you."

"What is it?"

"Can you track down a couple of people for me? I want to teach them a lesson," she says chillingly.

Chapter XIV

ADDICTIVE LOVE

"HELLO, RAINA!" A VOICE SAYS FROM BEHIND as she walks out of a patient's room. She turns and sees a big, burly young man with a straight face.

Raina stops and stares momentarily and asks, "Don't I know you from somewhere?"

He replies, "We were in high school together, but you probably don't remember me. I was only in school half the day since I was attending vocational school for welding. I was also on the football team my sophomore year, but I got in trouble with the law and was expelled. My name is Stuart McDowell."

"McDowell, McDowell…Are you related to Linda McDowell?"

Stuart nods. "That's my little sister."

"Okay, I remember you now. You were in the same class with me for English," replies Raina. "You just disappeared, but I do remember you being quiet."

"Everyone says that about me," he sheepishly replies, avoiding eye contact.

"I know this is probably a little rude of me to ask, but why were you expelled from school?" asks Raina.

"I was caught drinking a little hooch out in the football

stadium with a couple of friends that had already graduated. I made a bad mistake." He can only hold her gaze for a moment.

While listening to the very nice but timid young man, she realizes his naivety. She places her fingertips gently against his cheek and says, "I had a crush on you in school." She blushes. "We all make mistakes. You just learn from them and move on." She smiles and her eyes twinkle. "I'm about to go to lunch. If you're not busy, and if your girlfriend wouldn't mind, I would be flattered if you joined me."

Stuart's face lights up brightly as he replies, "Yes, I have time to have lunch with you. I don't have a girlfriend, though." He timidly shuffles his feet. "Can I ask you a question?"

"Yes, you can ask me anything."

"Do you have a boyfriend?" Stuart asks timidly.

Raina looks him in his eyes, waiting a moment before she answers, "Stuart, I can be available to a nice guy like you. Let me go clock out so we can talk."

"Okay," replies Stuart, a blush dusting his cheeks. Raina walks away, and a sinister half-smile pulls at her lips as she wonders how far he will go for her.

———

The rusted doors to the McDowell's barn in the backyard are partially slid open. Raina walks in and sees Stuart bent over under the hood of an old pickup truck. She can hear the rattling of metal tools. She sneaks behind him and says, "Hello, Stuart."

He jumps and hits his head on the raised hood of the truck. "Ow!" he yelps. He turns around, rubbing his head. "Raina, what are you doing here?"

"I'm here to see you, Stuart. You said I could come by anytime. Are you okay?" She walks up close to Stuart and puts her hand on the back of his head. "I don't feel any swelling up there," notes Raina.

Removing her hand, she turns to look at Stuart curiously. "What are you doing under the hood of that truck?"

"Huh?" It is quiet for a moment, then he snaps out of his daze. "Oh, I'm changing the spark plugs."

"Can I help?" asks Raina.

"A girl as pretty as you wants to work on a car? You'll get all dirty and sweaty."

"What's wrong with a girl working on a truck? There's nothing wrong with me getting a little dirty. I've worked with my father on his and my mother's car a few times. I've changed the oil in my own car before too." Her hands are on her hips as she walks up to the truck and picks up the wrench. "Well, get me a flashlight."

Stuart looks around and spots a flashlight on the nearby tool shelf. As he places it underneath Raina, she grins, "Okay, big guy, get yourself to the other side and pass me what I need."

"Yes, ma'am!" He laughs, astounded that she's working on an engine with him. He then asks, "Do you know how to weld too?"

"No, I don't," she replies.

"I work at US Pipe now as a welder, so I'm definitely glad I took those courses back in high school."

Raina catches Stuart's eye with a smile and says, "Cool! Maybe you can do some welding for me someday."

Stuart says, "Sure."

After finishing up on the truck, they walk back to the house. Stuart's parents are sitting on the back porch, and Stuart introduces her.

"Hello, Raina," greets Stuart's mother.

"Hi, Raina," says Stuart's dad. "Are you related to Attorney Willoughby?"

"Yes, sir!" Raina replies. "He's my father."

"He's a good man. He's represented a couple of people I work with in the coal mine," Mr. McDowell says.

"Dad, we're going in to wash up, then I guess Raina will be headed home." Stuart ends with slight hesitation in his voice.

Raina pipes up, "Stuart, I thought you were about to take me to the fairgrounds for the races." Raina winks at him.

"I was? Oh yeah, let's get going," replies Stuart with surprise.

Stuart's father says, "You seem like a very nice girl. Keep him out of trouble." He then smiles, looks at his son, and says, "Take care of her, and have a good time."

"Thanks, Dad! We will!" says Stuart,

After a fun day at the races, Raina and Stuart sit on the folded-down tailgate of his truck. Stuart breaks the silence, standing from the truck to face Raina, and says, "Raina, I have really enjoyed being with you tonight. You are so outgoing and funny."

Raina replies, "I'm just being myself. How did I make you feel?"

Stuart shyly averts his gaze for a moment then says, "It felt like you were my girlfriend. You held my hand, stood next to me, and you made me feel like you like me a lot." Stuart finishes by asking, expression earnest and adoring, "Raina, what do you see in me?"

Raina, still sitting on the back of the truck, gazes up at Stuart standing next to her. "Stuart, stand in front of me."

Stuart turns and stands in front of Raina. She opens her legs and says, "Come closer."

He steps up between her legs, and she puts her hands on his shoulders. "I see a big, strong, handsome man who wants me to be his girlfriend. So, you think I'm pretty, Stuart?"

He replies, star-struck, "Yes, Raina, you are the prettiest girl I have ever seen."

"Would you do anything to have me as your girlfriend?"

Stuart merely stares into Raina's eyes. She pulls his head down, kissing him softly, yet passionately.

When they lean away, he says, "Yes, I would do anything to have you as my girlfriend."

Raina pulls him toward her again and gently kisses him again on the lips then the cheek. She moves her lips up by his ear and says, "I want you to prove you really want me by doing something for me."

Stuart ask, "What is it?"

"Can you build me an A-frame?"

"Why—" Before he can finish his sentence, Raina presses her finger to his lips, then moves it to his cheek and places her lips on his, giving him a short kiss.

"Don't ask questions. Just do it for me, okay?" she requests in a sensual voice. Then she follows with, "Please?"

"Yes, I will do it for you."

———

Sunday morning, Raina arrives at church to find out that Reverend Doyle is no longer pastor of the church. Raina immediately leaves, heading over to his house.

When she arrives, the former pastor greets Raina with a hug and says, "It's so good to see you, Raina! Why aren't you at church, young lady?"

"I was told you were no long pastor of our church. Please, tell me that's not true!" Raina pleads.

Reverend Doyle, with a look of sadness, replies, "I was dismissed from my duties as pastor yesterday. The president of the trustee and deacon board came over yesterday and gave me the disappointing news. I can't talk about it, but I was wrongly accused. I'm very disappointed in a couple of the officials at the church, but they will reap what they sow." The good reverend's eyes water as he fights to hold the tears back.

Raina growls, "I hate them! I'm never going back there ever again."

"Raina, listen to me; never say you hate someone. You can be displeased with their actions, but remember the Lord said, 'Vengeance is mine.' Go back to church, Raina. There are good people there, and you are needed. All this will be straightened out, and I'll be back soon. Remember, good always prevails over evil," says Reverend Doyle as he reaches out and gives Raina a hug.

"Okay, love you!" Raina says with tears, trying to cheer up.

"Now, say a prayer for me," Reverend Doyle requests.

"I will," replies Raina as she gets back into her car. She drives slowly off, waving to the reverend, disappointment, sadness, and hurt on his face.

"Of all people, why did they do this to him?" Raina thinks.

The following week, the church announces that Elder Foster is the new senior pastor of the church.

"Raina, could you please drop off Reverend Doyle's robe at his house after school today?" Jacqueline asks as she passes Raina in the hallway, handing her the robe. "Someone found it in the choir room mixed in with their robes. I would take it by his house, but I have a meeting this evening after work."

Raina replies, "No problem. I will take care of it."

She takes it into her room and sits down on the bed, holding it, and thinks about some of the wonderful memories she has of the former pastor of the church. The time he came to one of her first tennis matches, attended her thirteenth birthday party, or the time he came by the hospital and read to her when she had her tonsils taken out. She thinks about their last conversation, the disappointment and hurt from this betrayal.

"I will get them back. I will get those platitude-quoting idiots."

Raina takes out a pair of scissors from her desk and begins cutting a long strip of material off from the bottom, goes into the sewing room, and sows a hem back around the lower section of the robe.

"Looks good as new!" says Raina. She holds up the strip of cloth from the robe and says, "Sometimes, you have to shove good down people's throats so nothing bad comes out of their mouths."

———

Raina turns off the main country road and drives about a mile down an old, dirt path to an abandoned church. She enters into the small foyer, pushing the creaking double doors open slowly into the sanctuary. As she walks down the middle aisle of the church, oak wooden pews lining each side, she looks around at the old stained-glass windows, admiring their beauty. The memories as a little girl visiting the church with Dora come back to her. The former church membership dwindled down over the years and eventually the church closed.

Raina walks past the pulpit into the back area of the church. As she walks down to the end of the hallway, Raina hears a female voice say, "Is someone out there? Help us, please!"

Raina slowly opens the last door on the right. There is a woman and a man sitting at a small, worn, wooden conference table. They both are bound to the steel-made chairs, cuffed at the ankles to the chair legs, and at the wrists to the arm rests. They are both duct-taped around their chests to the chair. The man has something in his mouth and a strip of tape across his lips, unable to speak.

"Nancy, that can't be you," gasps Mrs. Harriet James, the president of the finance committee of the Willoughby's church.

"Right church, wrong pew," wittily answers Raina. Raina looks over at the man sitting at the head of the table and smiles pleasantly, almost as if she were joining the two for a meeting. "Mr. Butler, how are you?" He can't respond, due to the tape across his lips.

"Oh, Raina, thank goodness you're here! Help us get out of these chairs now before that man comes back!" says Mrs. James in a frantic voice.

"You have nothing to worry about; my friend won't be back. He has no reason to come back," says Raina.

Walking fully into the room, she shuts the door behind her. Raina sits down at the table across from Mrs. James and asks, "Did you know someone falsely accused Reverend Doyle of adultery and theft?" She laughs. "Crazy, right? You wouldn't happen to have an idea of who that would be…" She pauses, looking deliberately between the two. "Would you?"

"Raina, get us out of here! Now!" yells Mrs. James.

"That's not important right now, Mrs. James. Now, I need to know why some of you were in cahoots against Reverend Doyle. Why was he falsely accused of stealing and adultery?" She removes her cloche hat and places it on the dusty table upside down.

Raina looks away from Mrs. James and over to Mr. Butler. "Why would anyone lie about a good man like Reverend Doyle? He is loved and respected by everyone. Was it because he didn't want to take the church in a direction that some of your old-mule fuddy-duddy buddies want it to go?"

Mrs. James outbursts, "Who do you think you are?! It's none of your business why we fired Reverend Doyle! Let us loose from these chairs right now!"

Raina replies in a no-nonsense tone of voice, "Mrs. James, could you please be quiet and speak when spoken to?"

Raina looks back at Mr. Butler and asks, "Mr. Butler, do you think I'm pretty?"

He hesitantly nods his head with fear in his eyes, trembling. Raina bat her eyelashes.

"Young lady! If you don't let us go right now, you are going to spend a long time in jail!" Mrs. James demands.

"Shut up, Mrs. James!" Raina stands up and walks over behind Mr. Butler, rests her hands on his shoulders, places her face next his, and asks, "Do you like the fragrance of my perfume?"

Mr. Butler moans twice against his gag and nods his head forward, agreeing.

Mrs. James screams, "Get us out of these shackles now! You listen here, young lady. I'm going to have you locked up for life once I get out of here!"

Raina raises her gaze and looks at Mrs. James maliciously, then her facial expression changes. Raina straightens up and walks back in front of Mrs. James. Pulling the derringer pistol out from behind her, she leans over the table and places the gun against Mrs. James forehead. "Two women can't stir the same pot," she says and pulls the trigger.

Mrs. James's head jerks back then forward. She's dead.

Raina places the gun on the table and looks at Mr. Butler, saying, "Sorry for the rude interruption. Now, where were we? Oh yes! Thanks for the compliments." Then, she reaches over and pulls the tape off his lips and pulls the ball of cloth out of Mr. Butler's mouth.

"Raina, I had nothing to do with Reverend Doyle. Please let me go. I promise I won't tell anyone. Please, don't kill me. Have some compassion," Mr. Butler begs, his voice quivering, drool running off his lips and down his chin, tears streaming down his face.

"So, you want compassion? The way I'm feeling right now, compassion better just hide and watch. Now, Mr. Butler, you have to be disciplined. You lied, and it was against a man of the cloth," she says.

Raina picks up the pistol and walks to Mrs. James' bloody and fallen corpse. Raina grabs a handful of her hair, jerking Mrs. James' head back, and says, "She is so much quieter dead."

"Help!" screams Mr. Butler over and over.

As he is screaming, Raina walks back over behind him and says, "No need to scream. No one can hear you. Let me sing you a song, so just relax." She puts her left hand on his shoulder and sings in her beautiful, angelic voice.

> *Them that's got shall get*
> *Them that's not shall lose*
> *so the Bible said and it still is news*
> *Mama may have, Papa may have*
> *But God bless the child that's got his own,*
> *that's got his own—*
> *Bang!*

———

Three hours later, Raina pulls off to the right side of a dirt road, next to a slim oak tree with a ribbon tied around its trunk. She gets out of the car, dark shades and a fall, cloche hat adorning her, closes the door, and looks to the trees and the sky.

She says, "What a lovely day!"

She walks about fifty yards down a dusty trail leading into the forest. From a distance, she sees her destination. A man is tied to a tree.

When Raina gets close to the person, she can see him

strapped to the tree with chains around his shins, thighs, waist, chest, and arms. Tape is wrapped around his forehead and the tree. His hands are tied behind the tree with handcuffs, and something is inserted in his mouth with a strip of tape across his lips, preventing him from talking. The man can only move his eyes.

Raina sits down on the stump of a tree about fifteen feet away from the man. She puts her hands on each side of the tree stump and crosses her legs. "Hello, Mr. Nelson. How are you?" Raina asks in a very proper voice with her brightest smile.

Mr. Nelson can only whimper as his eyes move frantically, pleading for help. Raina takes her shades off and puts them next to her on the tree stump. She stands up, wearing a tan blouse with brown pinstripes and brown pants that are tapered at her ankles. Brown shoes cover her feet, and a tan-trimmed brown cloche hat sits atop her head.

"Mr. Nelson, our church pastor of twenty-five years was terminated on charges of moral failure. In scripture, that would be Exodus 20:14. Let me explain what the charges are in plain terms: he is a thief and an adulterer," says Raina as she walks up and stands in front of Mr. Nelson.

"Now, we both know Reverend Doyle is a good man. He is well respected by everyone in the church and the community. He has done a great job of growing the church, with living and preaching the truth. You people found a way to get our phenomenal pastor fired," Raina utters as she steps back to the tree stump.

She then takes her cloche hat off and places it on the stump, her black hair glistening in the parted sunlight that's coming through the trees. As Mr. Nelson watches Raina walk back toward him, he moans, the sound muffled.

Raina stands in front of Mr. Nelson and just looks him in

the eyes with no expression on her face for about thirty seconds before saying, "You and the others lied about my pastor! You hurt him. He really loved pastoring our church." As Raina speaks, her emotions become more heated. "Reverend Doyle baptized me, he always supported me, and I could always go to him in confidence for direction. You hurt my pastor!" Raina yells.

Mr. Nelson whines and mewls, frantic to speak.

"Shut up, liar!" screams Raina as she swings and slaps Mr. Nelson across the face. She steps back a couple of feet, looking at the ground for a moment, then to the trees, then back at Mr. Nelson. Raina takes a couple of steps forward and stands directly in front of him.

Raina asks, "Mr. Nelson, do you think I'm pretty?"

Mr. Nelson gives two short groans, as if he's saying, "Uh-huh." She smiles.

Raina asks another question. "Do you like the fragrance of my perfume?" Again, Mr. Nelson moans an affirmative.

Raina steps back, still smiling, then her facial expression changes suddenly from delight to offence.

Raina reaches to her side with her right hand and pulls out a knife from a

dragon-printed holster.

"Mr. Nelson, what I'm holding in my hand is a Japanese knife. And quite a good one, as well. It's used to slice up fish," she explains as she holds the blade in front of Mr. Nelson, moving it around and appreciating its sharp edge and excellent workmanship. "This 11.8-inch blade has a unique trait: the single beveled edge. This knife is sharpened so that only one side holds the cutting edge and the other side remains flat. The flat edge is there so the meat doesn't stick to the knife," says Raina as she looks Mr. Nelson right in the eyes, a smirk overtaking her lips. Tears drip from Mr. Nelson's eyes as he whimpers in fear.

As Raina holds the knife in her right hand, the tips of her left-hand fingers rub its edge. "Mr. Nelson, do you know the legal definition of corporal punishment? I read a lot, so I'll tell you, just in case you don't know. It's a punishment for some violations of conduct which involves the infliction of pain on, or harm to, the body. Mr. Nelson, do you know that mutilation is an act of physical injury that degrades the appearance or function of any living body?"

Raina places the knife above Mr. Nelson's right ear, looks him directly in the eyes, and says, "Tell me how a filleted fish feels."

She pulls the knife down, slicing his ear off with ease, and it falls to the ground.

"Wow! This knife is sharper than I thought."

Mr. Nelson wails loudly in pain. His eyes are closed tightly, and blood runs down the side of his neck. Raina puts the knife in her opposite hand and slices his other ear off.

"You look different with no ears, Mr. Nelson," she says, laughing as Mr. Nelson sobs in pain, blood running down both sides of his face.

Raina takes the knife and puts it under his nose and says, "I can't cut your face. You're a handsome man." She winks at him.

Raina looks to the left of her shoulder, and in the blink of an eye, she turns back and looks into Mr. Nelson's eyes. She cuts his throat. As the blood runs down Mr. Nelson's chest, he gurgles, choking on his own blood, and Raina turns to her left again. There's a robin up in a nearby tree, looking at her.

Raina smiles and says to the bird, "This makes me happier than a black cat with a red bird in its mouth." As if the robin understands Raina, it quickly flies away.

She pulls a rag out of her back pocket and wipes the blood off the knife. She places the knife back in its holster then throws the rag on the ground. "Look at the blood on my favorite blouse. Good thing I brought another one to put on," remarks Raina. She walks over to the tree stump, picks up her hat, puts it on her head, then picks up her sunglasses and puts them on.

"Ah, what a lovely day out here in the country. *'One for my baby and one for the road...'*" she sings as she walks back down the path to her car.

Chapter XV

IT SHALL BE DONE

As Jacqueline walks into Raina's room, she smells a hint of the perfume Nancy used to wear. She has Nancy's old, red-flowered spread on her bed, hand-painted pictures of boats and lighthouses on the wall from Nancy's old house, and Nancy's boxed hats are placed neatly in her closet. She notices an opened book—a diary on closer inspection—on the vanity with a torn piece of newspaper inside. The paper is of Mr. Nelson from the obituary section of the newspaper.

Jacqueline picks up the article and looks down at the page in the book, which reads, "He cried, moaned, whimpered, I'm sure, begging for his life. The holy cloth in his mouth kept him from trying to manipulate and lie. Should a life be taken from a person who takes a life? Directly or indirectly? Well, I know one thing, I—"

Just then, the front door shuts, and Raina calls, "I'm home!"

Jacqueline looks up, startled, lays the article back down on the book, and walks out of Raina's room. Jacqueline heads downstairs, thinking of what she saw.

"Does she know something about these recent murders?"

Raina enters from a storm door and walks down through the alleyway into the damp and chilly courthouse basement. Water drips from the old pipes, and cobwebs line the walls. A musty smell runs along the room. Drips of water hit her gray cloche hat and the shoulders of her black jacket as she slowly walks.

There's a young woman standing on top of an old, wooden sitting stool with her hands tied behind her back and a noose snug around her neck. The rope is connected to a beam running along the ceiling. The girl has something in her mouth with a piece of tape across her lips.

"Chantel, how are you?" asks Raina as she walks up to Chantel, who is trembling in fear, knowing that if the chair tilts over, she will hang.

Raina stands directly in front of Chantel, looking up at her for a moment, then says, "I told you more than once that you were going to pay for that nasty attitude and your big mouth. You taunted and humiliated others, and myself, over the years. I thought you would grow up and change your nasty ways, but you only got worse."

Chantel shivers, both from fear and the cold.

"You think you're prettier than me, don't you?" asks Raina.

Chantel frantically shakes her head, and Raina bursts out and yells, "No!"

She turns to a corner packed with tools, most likely used for storage, and grabs a can of paint. She walks over and takes the flathead screwdriver off the top of the can and pries off the lid. She grabs a small paint brush, dips it in the paint, and grabs an empty bucket. She flips the bucket and places it in front of Chantel. She stands on it and draws an "X" on her face.

"No! You are not prettier than me!" shouts Raina.

Raina steps off the bucket and kicks it out of her way, looking up at Chantel with no expression on her face, then she smiles and says, "Chantel, you're a tough bird. I have a saying: the early bird gets the worm, but the second mouse gets the cheese."

Raina bends down and grabs the lower rail of the stool and pulls it out from under Chantel. She falls. Her body jerks for about seven seconds, suffocating from the hanging, then after about five minutes, she's close to dead.

Raina stands there for about fifteen minutes, looking directly at her. Raina lifts her right hand up and looks at her watch.

"You're pretty now—pretty dead," she says.

———

The phone rings, and it's reporter Roger Hayes from Jacqueline's newspaper.

"Jacqueline," he starts, voice small. "I have some bad news. Our mayor's daughter has just been found hanged in the basement of the courthouse."

"No!" she gasps. "It can't be! How could this have happened?" Tears run down her face. Sniffling, she continues, "I'm going over to the house to see Mary. I will call you back. Bye." She hangs up the phone and places her hands on her heart.

Jacqueline goes outside, where Raina is sitting on the back-porch swing, knitting a sweater.

"Raina, I have some bad news. Chantel is dead."

Before she can tell her what had happened, Raina looks at her with those beautiful, empty eyes. A terrible, hate-filled smile plays about her lips, and she says, "She deserved what happened to her."

"How could you say that? I know you didn't like Chantel, Raina, but I'm surprised you'd think that. I saw your book of newspaper articles about the people that have been killed lately. Is that what you think? That these people are getting what they deserved?"

Raina replies and looks straight ahead. "They all deserved
what they got." Then she turns to Jacqueline with chilling eyes
and continues, "Don't ever touch my diary again. Stay out of
my room."

Jacqueline, disturbed by her words, immediately leaves her.
Jacqueline puts her hat on and grabs her purse to go and help
comfort the mayor's wife, and her close friend, Mary.

———

Two months later, Inell's father wakes up in some abandoned
barn, miles out in the country.

"Where am I?" he asks. "What the hell?"

He realizes his wrists are handcuffed, ankles are shackled,
and he's standing, stretched forward, on an asymmetrical make-
shift ladder. He is shirtless, bent over across the connecting bar
of the ladder.

Mr. Howard looks forward, and Raina is sitting in a chair in
front of him, wearing a pair of Levi jeans, black-buckled leather
shoes, a black-ruffled blouse, and her black hair pinned up under her black-trimmed, white cloche hat. Her flawless lipstick
stretches over an inviting smile.

"Mr. Howard, how are you?" she asks.

"Raina!" he cries, scared and confused. "Where am I? What
the hell is going on?"

"Mr. Howard, you are a married man, correct?" asks Raina.

Mr. Howard screams, "You release me right now, young
lady! Get over here and take these handcuffs off me, right now!"

Raina's expression morphs into one of anger. She looks
right into Mr. Howard's eyes and says, "Where do you get off
talking to me like that, you adulterer? You are a married man,

Mr. Howard, so why do you run around on your wife? Why do you flaunt around with your girlfriends in other towns?"

Mr. Howard looks at Raina in disbelief. "Why are you doing this? What do you want? Money? Tell me what you want, and I well get it for you!" he begs.

As Raina reaches up with both hands and takes her black-trimmed cloche hat off, laying it down on the floor next to her chair, she pulls the pin out of her black hair. She's looking directly into Mr. Howard's eyes. Her wavy hair falls down to her shoulders.

Raina stands up, walks over to Mr. Howard, and bends down, level to his face. She asks seductively, softly, "Mr. Howard, do you think I'm pretty?"

Mr. Howard is shaking nervously, but a slight, conservative smile comes over his face, and he slowly nods. "Yes!"

Raina straightens and seductively unbuttons her blouse. She has a black wife-beater tee underneath. She slowly pulls the blouse off and drops it down to the floor with her left hand. Mr. Howard is looking at Raina's soft, light skin and her black hair laying on her shoulders.

"Mr. Howard," she purrs. "Do you like the fragrance of my perfume?" She then turns her face a little to the left and gets close enough to Mr. Howard that his nose touches her cheek. She lifts up slowly as his nose rubs down her cheek and her neck. As his nose touches her shoulder, she straightens up and steps back about four feet, looking him straight in his eyes with that sensual, inviting look on her face.

"Yes!" he replies, still shaking nervously.

In the blink of an eye, Raina's facial expression transforms to repulsed. Her face turns red as a cranberry. She rears her right arm back and slaps Mr. Howard in the face as hard as she can, then she repeats the action with her other hand, then again with the first. The slaps are so hard, it snaps his head each time.

He then screams, "What the hell is wrong with you!?" Drool runs from his mouth.

She immediately turns around, reaching into her pants pocket and pulling out a pair of gauntlet gloves to put on and walks to a wooden rack about twenty feet away in the barn.

Raina turns around with some sort of stick and returns to him. "Mr. Howard, do you know what this is?" asks Raina.

"No!" he yells. "And I really don't care what it is. You just get me out of these chains right now, young lady, or you will live to regret it," he loudly threatens.

"Well, Mr. Howard, this is a 3.9 foot long, half an inch-wide rattan cane that was given to me by my father. Pretty cool, huh, Mr. Howard? I read a book that said this cane is used for legal corporal punishment in Singapore. It's applied with such ferocity that the victims' buttocks are completely stripped of skin, leaving them raw and mutilated." She shifts her grip on the weapon. "Mr. Howard, a recipient of the cane described the pain as beyond excruciating," says Raina pleasantly.

Raina walks around to the side of Mr. Howard. "Please, don't do this! Please don't do this!" he blubbers.

Raina responds, "You should have thought about this when you were cheating on your wife! You should have thought about this when Inell was being taunted by the other girls in school on what an adulterer you are. You broke her heart when she found out her mother was divorcing you!"

The more Raina speaks, the louder her voice becomes. "You tried coming on to my mother Nancy several times when she would go shopping in the clothing store next to your office building. Do you remember coming on to me all those years ago at the library, Mr. Howard?"

Before Mr. Howard can speak, Raina, with rage in her

voice, interrupts, "Shut up, adulterer. You had me in the back corner of the library. You ran your old, nasty fingertips across my cheek and said, 'You're so pretty, and you smell good, too.' Luckily, my mother called, looking for me. I was sixteen years old, you pervert." She sneers.

Raina stops, closes her eyes, reopens them, and exhales a breath.

She raises the cane above her head as if it were a ninja sword, her legs spread apart and knees slightly bent. She waits a moment, then she swings.

She can hear the whistle of the cane in the air, coming down and striking Mr. Howard on his back. He screams out in pain as a half-inch wide, six-inch long section of skin is cut from his body by the rattan cane.

Raina then swings again, and Mr. Howard yells, "God, help me!"

By the fourth swing, Mr. Howard has passed out, skin ripped from his back and bloody.

Raina stops, black hair all over the place, sticking to her slightly sweaty face. She places the cane on the chair, taking her gloves off and placing them on top of the cane. Raina uses the front tail of her shirt to pat the sweat from her forehead, then bends down, taking the comb out of her sock. She combs her hair back in place before placing the comb back.

Appearance orderly again, Raina walks behind Mr. Howard and reaches for her pistol. She puts the gun to the back of Mr. Howard's head and pulls the trigger, shooting him once.

She puts the gun back in her back pocket, walks around to the front of Mr. Howard, grabs a handful of his hair, and pulls his head up, looking into his lifeless eyes and says, "You're officially now a retired hunk."

Raina then picks up her blouse, pulls it over her shoulders

and buttons it back up, twirls her hair and places the pin back in it, and puts her hat back on. She picks up the cane and gloves, looks back around, making sure nothing is left behind, and walks out of the barn. She gets into the car and drives back down the dirt road.

About five miles down the road, she stops on the little bridge over the rushing stream. She gets out of the car with the gloves and the cane, and she tosses them into the water. She stands there, watching the gloves go down stream as they begin to sink. Raina stands there for a moment with a slightly sinister smile on her face. She then gets back into the car and drives away.

———

As Jacqueline is about to start typing an article about the recent chain of murders in the city, she thinks about the people who were murdered. Some of them were close to the family, but all of them were known by Raina. She initially shakes the thought off, but Jacqueline has noticed the negative, strange comments and the distance since Nancy's death. She wonders if Raina knows anything about these deaths, especially after reading her diary page.

———

Four months later, as Attorney Jed Murphy awakens, he realizes he is outside in an open field.

"Where am I?" he asks as he looks around in confusion, shaking off the drug that had sedated him hours earlier. He tries moving his body, but notices he can't move his arms.

"Why am I in the ground?" He discovers that he is buried past his elbows, close to his shoulders.

"Attorney Murphy, how are you?" a voice from behind him asks.

"Who is that?" demands Murphy as he tries desperately to look behind him, but he can't. As he hears the steps walk around from behind and sees the two-tone, black-and-white saddle shoes stop in front of him, he looks up.

"Who are you?" he asks.

She stands in front of him in a t-shirt layered under a black-and-white checkered button-down shirt and a pair of loose-fit Levi jeans, with the legs rolled up to just below her knees. A small, black comb sticks halfway out of her right sock.

The person bends down on one knee and says, "I'm Raina. You defended the animal that killed Nancy Willoughby: Dr. James Posey." She spits on the ground as she stands up straight. "Attorney Murphy, do you know why you're here?"

"How did I get here?"

"As an attorney, you should know you never answer a question with a question," replies Raina.

As Murphy looks around, wondering what is going on, he says, "That guy last night must have put something in my drink." He pauses for a moment. "I don't know how I got here, but go get help, now!"

"I am your help, counselor," says Raina with a light smirk. "I'm going to release you as soon as we finish talking."

"Get me out of this hole, girl! Stop playing games with me, and help me out of here, now!" yells Murphy, rage steaming across his face.

"You said 'games?' Let's play a game." Raina kneels down on one knee about six feet away from Murphy, then draws a two-foot-wide circle on the ground with her finger. She pulls seven marbles out of her pocket and places five of them in the circle. She places one of the two larger marbles in front of Murphy and moves back a couple of feet. "You ever played marbles, counselor?"

"What do you mean? Get me out of this hole, now!" he screams. "Do you know who I am? I have pull in this city! I will have you locked up and the key thrown away if you don't get me out of here!"

Raina stands up and walks behind him. She picks up a roll of tape, tears off an eight-inch strip, and bends down in front of him. "You're like some lawyers I've been around—just can't keep that flap you call a mouth shut." She puts the tape across his lips. "Now we can concentrate on this game of marbles."

Raina walks back to the marbles, kneels down outside the ring, and flicks the shooter marble out of her fist with her thumb. She hits two of the marbles out of the ring. With each shot, she moves around the circle, kneels down, shoots, and knocks out a marble. After four shots, all five marbles are outside of the circle.

Raina walks around and picks up all five marbles. "Not bad for a twenty-year-old girl who hasn't shot marbles in a few years, huh, counselor?"

Attorney Murphy's face is red, his veins standing out in his neck and forehead from the built-up anger and his inability to speak.

Raina walks over and picks up the shooter marble in front of Murphy. "You won't be needing this," she says as she places all seven marbles back in her pants pocket.

"Now, back to business. Attorney Murphy, you are here today because you assisted in freeing a known abuser and murderer," says Raina. "You are sworn to uphold justice in the courtroom, but you chose to lie, cheat, disgrace reputations and honor, and make a mockery of the judicial system. When I heard Judge Roberts had died, I thought, you know who would be a better candidate to fill his grave? You, Attorney Murphy."

Raina kneels down on one knee, smiles, and asks, "Attorney Murphy, do you think I'm pretty?"

Murphy moans and shakes his head in anger.

"I'll take that as a 'yes,'" says Raina as she blushes. She leans forward, placing her face near the side of his, and asks, "Do you like the fragrance of my perfume?"

Murphy groans loudly, trying to scream, his face red as a pepper.

"I'll take that as a 'yes,' too," says Raina. She stands up. "It's time for your punishment, Attorney Murphy. I told you I was going to release you—release you from this life."

Raina walks over to a pile of white stone gravel rocks as big as baseballs, about ten feet away. "Attorney Murphy, have you ever heard of lapidation, or stoning? In case you don't know, it's a practice of capital punishment whereby a group throws stones at a person until they die. The reason it's done in a group is so no individual among the group can be singled out as the one who kills the subject."

Raina bounces one of the rocks in her hand and looks around. "No group here, so I guess I'll be the individual who kills the subject."

Murphy whimpers and shakes his head frantically as tears run down his face.

Then her face darkens, her mouth pulling up into a twisted smile. Justice was the right thing. Always. "Sometimes, there's no forgiveness to be found. Especially for someone like you. At-torney Murphy, I would suggest you close your eyes and say a prayer, because this is going to hurt. I'll give you a moment," she says, then bows her head for a few seconds.

"Okay, show time!" Raina reaches around her back and pulls out an old, worn Barons baseball cap—and puts it on her head.

She takes the first gravel rock, winds up like a pitcher, and throws it. It hits the side of the attorney's face hard, and he moans in pain. The second rock hits him in the nose, causing blood to come rushing down over the tape across his lips. The third rock hits his forehead; the fourth hits his mouth.

Raina throws the sharp-edged gravel rocks one after another as hard as she can, each one landing against the face and head of the attorney until he is almost unconscious. After Raina throws the fifteenth rock, she just stands there, looking at him.

Then, she takes the baseball cap off and places it back in her pants pocket. She uses the sleeve of her shirt to wipe the sweat off her forehead, then reaches down to get her comb out of her sock. She takes a moment to comb her hair back in place, putting the comb back in her sock once she's finished.

She walks up to the badly bruised and bloody attorney and says, "You, along with the others, killed my mother. The stoning was for my satisfaction, the game of marbles was just for entertainment, but this bullet to your head is for her."

Raina reaches around and takes the derringer pistol out of her back pocket. She places it against the top of the attorney's head, closes her eyes, and pulls the trigger.

Chapter XVI

IT MAY BE THE LAST TIME,
I DON'T KNOW

A T THE BIRMINGHAM AIRPORT, Raina sits in the waiting area for her flight to Boston to board.

"Flight 6762 to Boston is now ready to board." She hears over the airport terminal intercom.

Raina stands and says to herself, "There's an old Latin proverb that says, 'Revenge is a confession of pain.' Well, I'm hurting really badly, so let me visit the doctor and fill the prescription he wrote."

———

"Hello, Dr. Posey. How are you?" Raina asks as the doctor returns to consciousness. She sits next to the bed with her legs crossed and a small book in her hand named *Consequences of Life* by Shawn Crawford.

The doctor looks at Raina, quickly blinking to clear his eyes, and asks, "Nancy?"

Raina places the book down in her lap and says, "Right school, wrong class. I'm Raina, Nancy's daughter." She tilts her head. "You remember me, don't you?"

Dr. Posey tries to get up but quickly realizes his hands and feet are cuffed and chained to each side of the bed. There are straps across his body, tying him to the bed.

"What is going on here? Why am I tied down?" he asks, straining to look around, as he is only able to move his head. "That guy that came to my door and asked to use my telephone must have knocked me out when I turned my back. I have a terrible headache," he continues.

"Dr. Posey, I'm here to ask you a couple of questions. First, why did you assault my mother?" Raina asks in a calm, composed voice.

Dr. Posey lays his head back down on the pillow and looks up at the ceiling. "I didn't mean to hurt her," he swears as tears run down the side of his temples. "When she slapped me, I just got so mad. I couldn't control myself! I tried, but something inside me won't let me stop!" he says in an uncontrollable cry.

Raina stands up from the chair and walks around the very nicely decorated bedroom, slowly looking at the pictures on the wall. She stops in front of the bedroom window, moving the curtain slightly, and gazes outside into the dark, chilly night.

She turns and looks at the doctor, unable to move his body, securely chained and strapped to his king-size bed. Raina asks, "Dr. Posey, what do you not understand about the word 'stop?' My momma asked, pleaded, and begged for you to stop hurting her. I yelled at you to stop hurting her, but you hit me, and that's all I remember until I came to. And my mother was on the floor, beaten in her own home!" yells Raina as her face distorts with rage.

She looks away from Dr. Posey and closes her eyes to compose herself. She then walks across the room back to the bedside of the crying doctor and says, "Now, now, Dr. Posey, there's no need to cry." She smiles, taking a handkerchief out of her pocket and wiping away tears from his eyes.

"I have just two more questions for you. The first: do you think I'm pretty?" Raina asks.

The doctor replies, sweating and trembling, "Yes, you are just as beautiful as your mother."

Raina smiles then leans forward and puts the side of her face close to his nose and asks, "The second: do you like the fragrance of my perfume?"

"Yes."

Raina stands up straight, reaches back and slaps him across the face. "That was for me." She reaches back and slaps him again, saying, "That was another one for me!" Raina steps back and says, "You just couldn't stop until you finally killed my momma. You should have been in prison where you belong, and she would still be alive."

Raina stands at the foot of the bed and says, "I sat in that courtroom, knowing that the judge would put you behind bars, but low and behold, your daddy paid his old friend the judge to keep your butt out of prison. I thought that the justice system was fair, but it's not. The people that have the power to taint those sworn to uphold the system are the problem."

Dr. Posey lays on the bed with an expression of worry and regret on his face and says, "Release me. Release me now!" He frantically begins to pull and tug at the restraints.

He sees Raina step out of the bedroom and into the hallway for a moment, then return with a pair of gloves on, holding a metal half-gallon container.

She takes the cap off and begins dousing kerosene on the doctor from his waist down and around the bed.

When Raina finishes dousing the kerosene, she rests the container next to the bed and says, "Now, now, big bad wolf, all that huffing and puffing isn't going to save you. Do you know how my momma felt when you held her down against her will? She was helpless against something she didn't want to happen. If you don't know, now you do, doctor. I have one more thing to say…Go back to hell!"

Raina strikes the match and throws it on top of the doctor, which ignites a fire over his waist and legs. He screams and cries out slurs as the fire burns on and around him.

Raina walks down the spiral staircase, dragging her hand along the cherry hand-railing and admiring the nicely decorated home. She walks through the living room area over into the kitchen. Once she enters the kitchen, she turns on all four burners to the gas stove and the oven.

She walks over to the kitchen counter where an oil lamp sits, and she raises the glass cover and lights the flint, putting the glass cover back in place. The screams have died down from upstairs. Raina takes her gloves off and lays them down on the counter next to the burning lamp. She picks up his car keys off the counter, walks out the back door of the kitchen, and gets into the doctor's car, starting it up.

She looks up at the house that will soon be engulfed with fire, backs the car out of the driveway, goes down the street about four blocks, then turns the car around to face the house. A few minutes later, it happens: *kaboom!*

The windows of the lower level blow out, followed by flames and thick smoke. Raina can see Dr. Posey's bedroom window as bright as the sun, obviously filled with fire. The house is burning out of control.

Raina starts the car back up, and just before she drives off, she says with a smirk, "He nor the demon in him will hurt anyone else." She then drives away.

—

About three weeks later, Concepción strolls up to the Willough-by home.

"Hi, Miss Dora!"

Dora opens the screen door, letting the young woman in. "How are you doing this fine day?" asks Dora.

"I'm doing pretty well, Miss Dora. I stopped by to ask Raina if I could borrow a hat for church tomorrow," replies Concepción, already walking up to Raina's room.

"She's not here right now, but go on up and get whichever one you need. She's got a ton of them anyway," says Dora as she laughs, continuing her clean of the living room floor.

"Okay, Miss Dora. Thanks!"

Once inside, Concepción rifles through the closet and looks into the different hat boxes to find the right one for her new Sunday dress.

She opens one of the boxes and lifts the hat up, saying, "Nice look, but the color is wrong."

As she starts to put the hat back in the box, she notices a small, brown book under the white tissue paper in the bottom of the box.

"What's this?" Concepción mutters.

Concepción's facial expression changes from one of intrigue to disturbance.

She slowly walks over to Raina's desk and sits down, reading the book with a troubled look on her face. She flips forward through the pages, tears threatening to fall.

She puts her hand over her mouth, her body trembling, as tears run down her face. "Oh my god!" she exclaims as she reads the last written page in the book. "No, Raina!"

Concepción runs out of Raina's room, leaving the book opened on the desk. She rushes down the stairs, through the living room, and out the front door, getting into her car and speeding away.

Dora walks up to the living room window and says, "What has gotten into that girl?" She goes back to waxing the floor.

———

Alexander asks Raina to meet him so they can talk.

"I can't keep doing this Raina," he cries. "I'm kidnapping people, and you're killing them. You said you were only going to scare them, but you killed all of them. I'm an accessory to the murders you're committing. You're hurting their families because you think they had something to do with your mother's death or because you're angry at them." He nervously shakes. "This is so wrong."

"We are killing these people because they are bad. They are bad people that don't deserve to live," she decrees, looking at him with fire in her eyes. She whirls on him. "You're not going to quit on me! You said that you would do anything for me! You said you loved me!"

Raina puts her arms around him and lays her face on his shoulder. After a few moments, she raises her head back up and kisses him softly on his lips. "Do this last one for me?"

He stands there, looking into Raina's eyes with tears running down his face, figure trembling, and he timidly says, "No, Raina, I can't do it. I can't put another person in place for you to kill."

Raina stiffens then holds him close to her with a warm, tight hug. She reaches around to her back and pulls out the derringer pistol with her right hand. She releases her hug, and her expression darkens. She says in a firm voice, "You just broke my heart." She quickly raises her right arm up and places the pistol to his temple.

From a short distance away, Concepción screams, "No, Raina!"

She pulls the trigger, and Alexander falls to the ground. Blood splatters on her face, and she turns around, placing the gun to her side.

Concepción runs up to Raina, crying, and screams, "Why!? Why did you kill him!?"

"He was weak, Concepción," she says chillingly.

"Sis," she gasps. "Why did you kill those people?! Why did you have Alexander kidnap them?"

"That's what he did as a soldier in the war. That's what he was trained to do." Raina pauses and gazes at Concepción fully. "How do you know about this, Concepción?"

"Because I just left your house. I went up to your room to borrow a hat and found your diary. My best friend is a killer." A choked sob escapes her. "Why, Raina? Please tell me!"

"What don't you understand, Concepción?!" she yells. "Those people killed my mother and badly hurt my friends and me. I treated them with respect and kindness, but they took my kindness and generosity for weakness. They were jealous of my talents, looks, perfumes, and clothes. Damn them, Concepción, damn them!" Her scream is raw.

"Who do you think you are? Some people are going to say bad things to you, they're going to hurt your feelings, they're going to piss you off, and, yes, Raina, some people are going to be jealous, but that's not a reason to kill them! You're sick, Raina! I don't know who you are anymore! I have to tell someone about this. I can't stand by and let you kill anyone else."

"Concepción! You're not going to tell anyone anything," she warns.

Concepción turns to walk away, but Raina grabs her blouse sleeve. Concepción turns around and slaps Raina in the face, causing her to stumble back. Concepción stands there, looking down at the madness in Raina's face with fire in her eyes.

Raina stands up straight about five feet away from Concepción, the right side of her face now sporting a red bruise. Raina, still holding the derringer pistol, extends her arm and aims for Concepción's heart.

"You just hurt me," Raina says as she squeezes the trigger. *Click!* Both Raina and Concepción flinch, but they both are still standing, looking at each other.

Raina doesn't not have a second bullet in the gun. At this realization, Concepción runs forward and swings a fist with all her might. She strikes Raina in the face, and she drops the pistol

The fight is on.

The young ladies clash, each girl pushing and pulling, tussling and hitting. They bump into a couple of trees around them. Concepción trips over a tree branch, pulling Raina down with her. Raina, on top of Concepción, hits her in the face. She pauses, reaching over to pick up a large rock. Concepción takes this chance to pull out Raina's long hair pin. She jabs it into Raina's shoulder, and Raina screams, dropping the rock. Raina falls off her, and Concepción lunges for the pistol and runs. Raina is laying on the ground, a hand around the long pin, trying to pull it out of her shoulder.

———

Two hours later, the police chief Andrew Pope knocks on the Willoughby's door. Frank answers. "Hi, Chief Pope. What are you doing here?"

"I'm sorry to inform you, but I have an arrest warrant for your daughter Raina for the murder of Alexander Mitchell among others that took place over the last year." He looks regretful.

"There has to be some mistake," replies Frank with a shake of his head.

"I wish it was. I'm as shocked as you are about this. We have a witness who may have seen Raina kill Alexander. Frank, we also have a detailed written confession that was mailed to me from Alexander explaining how he was the accessory to some of the murders Raina allegedly committed. I checked out everything that was stated in the letter. I regret to say that we have all the evidence to serve the arrest warrant."

As Pope and Frank talk, Jacqueline is standing at the front door with Dora behind her, wondering what is going on. Jacqueline walks out on to the porch and stands next to Frank.

"Please let me speak with my daughter, and I will bring her down to the station so she can turn herself in, and we can get this mistake straightened out," pleads Frank. "Please, Andy."

He sighs. "Okay, we'll be looking for you at the station soon."

"Thanks, old friend."

As Dora approaches Raina's bedroom door, she thinks, "Right now, this girl needs somebody." She knocks on Raina's bedroom door before opening it. Raina is sitting at the foot of her bed, staring out the bedroom window to the beautiful view of the forest behind the house. Her hands are flat on her thighs as she sits perfectly straight, gaze blank. Her blouse and skirt are dirty, and blood stains the right arm of her blouse. Dora walks over slowly and sits next to the young lady she helped raise. She looks out the window, too, then reaches over and places her hand on top of Raina's.

Raina looks over at Dora and lays her head on her shoulder. Dora says, "Everything's gonna be alright."

—

Three of the best lawyers in the state represent Raina in court. Also, the defense proves that all the stress Raina received over time due to the assault on her and her mother and the loss of her mother brought on the behavior. The doctors diagnose Raina with hysteria. Raina is found not guilty of the murders by reason of insanity and acquitted, but she is confined to the Bryce Psychiatric Hospital in Tuscaloosa.

After Raina is sent to Bryce Hospital, Jacqueline is packing up some of Raina's books to take down to her when she finds Raina's diary again.

Two years later, Jacqueline writes about this event, slightly altering names and murders to create her first fiction book, and gives it to a family friend that owns a local small publishing company. He prints up a few books that were proofs and ships them to her. Jacqueline comes home one evening and sees Frank cutting up the books.

Jacqueline asks, "What are you doing? Why are you cutting up my books?"

He replies frantically, "What are you trying to do to this family name, our reputations?"

"What are you talking about?"

Frank picks up the manuscript off the desk and says, "This! You are trying to destroy our family name. I also went down to the publisher and took care of everything down there."

"No, Frank, the books you have destroyed are not the same as the manuscript in your hand."

Frank destroys the one unedited manuscript and two sets of printing plates. There were twelve books printed from a second edited manuscript, eight of which Frank destroyed in the family room. The remaining four books and the second manuscript were in Jacqueline's office back at the newspaper. Those four books and manuscript disappeared from the bottom of her desk drawer. But there was only one book printed from the manuscript that Frank destroyed with the full unedited truth about Raina, explaining why there was a second set of printing plates. That book was hidden in with the other books in the Willoughby's family study.

A couple of years later, the book *Jacqueline Willoughby* is found at an elementary school across town. One of the kids, Dora's grandson, found it in the Willoughby's bookcase and took it for show and tell. Jacqueline gets wind of the book and enquires about it, but a gentleman with red hair and beard claims the book—Francis Laurent.

Almost seven years of trying to get Raina out of the hospital, the team of attorneys go in front of a judge, asking for Raina to be released.

The laws that govern the practice of committing people who are acquitted because of mental illness dictate that they be hospitalized until they're deemed safe to be released to the public, no matter how long it takes.

The judge reviews all the evidence, testimonies, and letters requesting Raina's release. The judge was sympathetic and finally rules in her favor, and Raina is to be released from the hospital in thirty days.

Jacqueline turns off the main street and circles around in front of the hospital to park, where she sees Raina sitting in a chair under the tulip poplar tree with her legs crossed, sunglasses on, and reading a book. Jacqueline signs in at the front desk and walks across the lawn, taking a folding chair along with her.

The two hug, sit down, and talk about plans for Raina's return home, but Raina wants a fresh start, so she decides to move out of the state. She was always wise with her money, and Nancy left her financially well, so she'll have enough to move. Frank and Jacqueline will give her whatever she needs, though.

"Where are you going to live?"

"The best place to reinvent the wheel: Buffalo, New York."

"Why Buffalo?" asks Jacqueline.

"I've always wanted to visit Niagara Falls. And I've read that Buffalo is known for its entertainment, fine dining, and wonderful shopping—a place where I can start my life all over again."

Raina then follows with, "But guess who came and paid me a visit?"

Jacqueline smiles. "I don't know. Who?"

Raina grins. "My father, Francis."

Jacqueline's eyes widen, and she asks, "Really? When did you see him?"

"He came last Sunday. Mother, we spent the whole day together. What a wonderful man! We shared each other's life stories. He told me about how my mom and he met, and how he held me as a baby. He also attended some of my high school tennis matches, and he was at my high school graduation. He was around at times, and we never knew it. He asked if I would forgive him for leaving us. I told him I couldn't *not* forgive him, but he insisted on hearing those words: I forgive you. He told me why he left Birmingham. It all started back in 1922..."

To be continued...

www.ingramcontent.com/pod-product-compliance
Lightning Source LLC
Chambersburg PA
CBHW030610130626
46552CB00017B/354